Be sure to look up the reading group discussion
questions at the end of the book!

* * *

Jake edged closer and cupped her cheek.

His callused thumb made a small, circular motion
on her skin that set Maggie's senses swirling. His
gaze snagged hers and threatened never to let go.

"You're my best friend, Maggie," he murmured.

His hand slowly lowered, and Maggie fought the
compulsion to reach for his wrist and hold it in
place. Instead, she took a step back.

"You're the best friend I have, too," she said. And
she meant it.

But best friends didn't make each other go weak in
the knees. Didn't make them contemplate things
best left alone.

Did they?

What was a best friend to do?

Dear Reader,

Not only does Special Edition bring you the joys of life, love and family—but we also capitalize on our authors' many talents in storytelling. In our spotlight, Christine Rimmer's exciting new miniseries, VIKING BRIDES, is the epitome of innovative reading. The first book, *The Reluctant Princess,* details the transformation of an everyday woman to glorious royal—with a Viking lover to match! Christine tells us, "For several years, I've dreamed of creating a modern-day country where the ways of the legendary Norsemen would still hold sway. I imagined what fun it would be to match up the most macho of men, the Vikings, with contemporary American heroines. Oh, the culture clash—oh, the lovely potential for lots of romantic fireworks! This dream became VIKING BRIDES." Don't miss this fabulous series!

Our Readers' Ring selection is Judy Duarte's *Almost Perfect,* a darling tale of how good friends fall in love as they join forces to raise two orphaned kids. This one will get you talking! Next, Gina Wilkins delights us with *Faith, Hope and Family,* in which a tormented heroine returns to save her family and faces the man she's always loved. You'll love Elizabeth Harbison's *Midnight Cravings,* in which a sassy publicist and a small-town police chief fall hard for each other and give in to a sizzling attraction.

The Unexpected Wedding Guest, by Patricia McLinn, brings together an unlikely couple who share an unexpected kiss. Newcomer to Special Edition Kate Welsh is no stranger to fresh plot twists, in *Substitute Daddy,* in which a heroine carries her deceased twin's baby and has feelings for the last man on earth she should love—her snooty brother-in-law.

As you can see, we have a story for every reader's taste. Stay tuned next month for six more top picks from Special Edition!

Sincerely,

Karen Taylor Richman
Senior Editor

Please address questions and book requests to:
Silhouette Reader Service
U.S.: 3010 Walden Ave., P.O. Box 1325, Buffalo, NY 14269
Canadian: P.O. Box 609, Fort Erie, Ont. L2A 5X3

Almost Perfect

JUDY DUARTE

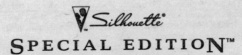

SPECIAL EDITION™

Published by Silhouette Books

America's Publisher of Contemporary Romance

To my editor, Stacy Boyd. Your support and keen
editorial eye make me want to reach higher and dig
deeper. A simple thank-you doesn't seem to be enough.

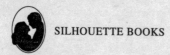 SILHOUETTE BOOKS

ISBN 0-373-24540-8

ALMOST PERFECT

Copyright © 2003 by Judy Duarte

Visit Silhouette at www.eHarlequin.com

Printed in U.S.A.

Books by Judy Duarte

Silhouette Special Edition

Cowboy Courage #1458
Family Practice #1511
Almost Perfect #1540

JUDY DUARTE,

an avid reader who enjoys a happy ending, always wanted to write books of her own. One day, she decided to make that dream come true. Five years and six manuscripts later, she sold her first book to Silhouette Special Edition.

Her unpublished stories have won the Emily and the Orange Rose awards, and in 2001, she became a double Golden Heart finalist. Judy credits her success to Romance Writers of America and two wonderful critique partners, Sheri WhiteFeather and Crystal Green, both of whom write for Silhouette.

At times, when a stubborn hero and a headstrong heroine claim her undivided attention, she and her family are thankful for fast food, pizza delivery and video games. When she's not at the keyboard or in a Walter Mitty–type world, she enjoys traveling, romantic evenings with her personal hero and playing board games with her kids.

Judy lives in Southern California and loves to hear from her readers. You may write to her at: P.O. Box 498, San Luis Rey, CA 92068-0498. You can also visit her Web site at: www.judyduarte.com.

Dear Reader,

I'm honored to have *Almost Perfect* chosen as the May Readers' Ring release. For those of us who love reading books and enjoy discussing them, the Readers' Ring is a great way to further our pleasure and understanding of stories with emotionally compelling plots and characters.

Almost Perfect holds a special place in my heart, in part because Maggie and Jake became so real in the writing process. And, yes, maybe because there's a little bit of Maggie in me.

As teenage friends, Maggie and Jake had similar backgrounds, yet different ways of coping with their past. Isn't that the way it is for all of us? We make choices, sometimes conscious and sometimes not, based upon our personal histories and experiences. And as humans, we hate to make changes in our lives unless forced by circumstances oftentimes out of our control.

No matter how difficult the problem, I want my characters to learn that when a door closes they should look for an open window. There is always a way out of even the worst place, but sometimes a person has to work to get there. I hope Maggie and Jake's story inspires you to remember that, too!

Happy reading,

Judy Duarte

Chapter One

Way back in third grade, Jake Meredith decided that only a complete fool would set himself up for failure. Thank God he'd learned that lesson early on.

It was a game plan that had served him well over the years.

Until fate threw him a curve.

Surveying the barn and corrals, Jake stood at the kitchen sink of the main ranch house and shook his head. *Buckaroo Ranch. What a waste of good land and stock.*

He'd had his fill of this place years ago and left home on his eighteenth birthday. But now, in spite of his distaste for city slickers and dude ranches, the whole kit and caboodle was his.

And since his sister had taken deposits for reservations a year in advance, and he didn't have a clue what she'd done with the money, he was stuck running the place until the guests had a chance to play cowboy for a week.

But that wasn't the bulk of his problems.

He glanced across the kitchen at the eighteen-month-old boy who was making a godawful mess with his bowl of spaghetti. When their eyes met, the toddler flashed a big grin, oozing with red-tinged slobber. Jake wasn't sure whether Sam was pleased with the taste of marinara or just plain happy to smear sauce and noodles in his hair and all over the high chair.

Rosa was going to have a hell of a mess to clean up, but she wouldn't complain. She never did. He supposed the nanny loved Kayla and Sam like her own children, which was lucky for them.

Not that Jake didn't love his niece and nephew, he did. They were the neatest kids he'd ever known, and he had always indulged them like a good uncle should. But one day, the girl and boy who adored him would learn he was a fraud—something they were bound to find out soon, now that he was their full-time guardian.

He took one last look at the court documents that had just arrived, the legal ruling that sealed the fates of his sister's kids, as well as his own. He shoved the papers back into the manila envelope and tossed the whole legal package on top of the fridge—out of sight, but certainly not out of mind.

Jake combed a hand through his hair. He wasn't any good at family stuff. Never had been. Hell, everyone he'd ever loved had failed him, one way or another. Even Sharon, his sister, who'd died and left him in a lurch.

When he and Sharon were kids, she'd tried to look out for him, to keep him on the straight and narrow. He'd grumbled and complained about her nagging, of course, but it had been comforting to know she loved him in spite of his rebellious nature. And that she'd always be there for him.

Times like today, when things were really piling up on him, he would always touch base with his sister. Dying wasn't her fault, but he'd felt deserted, just the same.

Of course, he'd come up pretty damn short on the dependability scale himself. He'd never been one to check in with his sister on a regular basis, so by the time Rosa finally tracked him down at a rodeo in Wyoming and relayed the grim news of the car accident, it was too late to attend the funeral services for Sharon or her husband.

The phone rang, interrupting his thoughts. He snatched the receiver from the wall. "Hello."

A woman's voice on the other end seemed to stutter and falter. "Jake?"

"Yeah?"

"It's me, Maggie."

Thoughts of Maggie Templeton brought a slow smile to his lips. In his mind, she was still seventeen, tall and awkward, with hair the color of corn silk and a splatter of freckles across her nose. As a teenager, she'd been the best friend he'd ever had. His only friend, he supposed.

They hadn't seen each other in fifteen years, but they talked on the telephone periodically, catching up on major life events like marriage, divorce and death.

"How are you doing?" she asked.

Jake looked at five-year-old Kayla, then at Sam. What was he going to say in front of the kids? That he was struggling to be the kind of father his sister would want him to be? That he was scared spitless he wouldn't measure up? "I'm doing okay."

"Is Rosa still working for you?"

Jake didn't know what he'd do without the woman who'd taken care of Sharon's kids since birth. Rosa wasn't just his baby-sitter, housekeeper, office manager and reader of bedtime stories; she was a blessed saint. "I doubled her salary, just to make sure she wouldn't quit."

"That's great," Maggie said. "I…uh…" She seemed to hesitate over the words, so he waited for her to speak. For a moment he thought the line had disconnected.

"You what?"

She blew out a sigh. "I need a date on Saturday night. And I thought that, if I purchased your airline ticket, you might come help me out."

"Be your date?" He couldn't keep the surprise out of his voice.

"Yes. As a favor to me."

It wasn't like Maggie to ask for help, and he figured this phone call hadn't been easy to make. "Are you still living in Boston?"

"For the time being. I'm going to be moving to California in a couple of months."

Something didn't add up. He'd never been one to pry, although he did wonder about the details. "Don't they have any eligible men in Boston? Why are you asking *me?*"

"Because I want a friend to escort me to a benefit dance, and I can't think of anyone else I'd rather go with."

Jake glanced at the Spaghetti Kid, just as Sam chucked a Melmac plate across the kitchen, littering the floor with noodles and splatters of sauce. Several strands of pasta dangled from his downy-fine hair, and Jake couldn't help shaking his head and smiling at the happy little boy.

At the kitchen table, five-year-old Kayla slowly sucked a long string of spaghetti into her mouth while concentrating on a picture book illustration of a bunch of roller-skating bugs parading through a strawberry patch. She'd been grumpy when he wouldn't read to her and Sam while they ate, something Rosa often did.

But Jake refused to read out loud. It put too damn much pressure on him to perform, and it brought back too many memories of childhood.

He looked at the spaghetti-riddled floor. Escaping Texas and going to Boston for a day or two suddenly sounded very appealing. "Okay."

"Are you sure? What about the kids?" she asked.

"Rosa's good with them, and they love her. Shoot, she's already raised three boys and a girl." Sam and Kayla were far better off with Rosa than a bachelor uncle who didn't know squat about kids.

"You're sure you don't mind?"

Mind getting away? Mind seeing Maggie again? "Not at all. I'll line things up around here, then let you know what time my flight arrives."

Dr. Maggie Templeton paced in front of the walkway that led to the terminal gate. What made her think she could call a man out of the blue and ask him to do a favor like this?

Desperation, that's what. And a hospital benefit she didn't want to attend.

Maybe she should have feigned an attack of appendicitis. Or put a cast on her leg. She could have called the dentist and scheduled an unnecessary root canal. How was that for desperation?

She blew out a ragged breath. No matter how plausible the excuse, it didn't matter. Dr. Margaret Templeton would arrive on time, dressed to the hilt, looking comfortable on the outside, while childish insecurities ran amok on the inside. At least she'd have Jake at her side.

But Maggie wasn't sure that seeing him again would make her feel any more secure.

A voice over the intercom announced his plane had arrived from Houston, and her steps faltered.

He was here. Would she recognize him after all these years?

Maggie stood transfixed, searching the steady stream of disembarking passengers for someone who resembled the gangly teenager who'd once been her best friend.

Did he still wear his hair long and slightly unkempt? Had he finally grown taller than her? Did he still prefer Wrangler jeans, a worn Stetson and scuffed boots?

As a tall, lean cowboy, dressed in black, sauntered through the door, her breath caught. *Jake?*

Bright blue eyes, the color of a Texas summer sky, crinkled in amusement, and he flashed her a reckless smile. "Hot damn, Maggie. You grew up good."

"So did you," she managed to say.

Jake Meredith now stood six-two or more, broad at the shoulders and narrow at the hips. Sporting a black suede jacket and Stetson, the man caused more than one head to turn for a double take.

He hadn't shaved this morning, she noticed, but the dark stubble looked good, giving him an intriguing, rugged appearance—a look even her most conservative side found appealing.

A small, jagged scar marred his left brow. The physician in her wondered how it had happened.

The woman in her wanted to trace it with her finger.

Whoa, she told herself, pulling out of the awkward trance. Jake was her friend, her escort. She had no intention of stretching their relationship beyond that. Sharon, his sister, had said he was a charmer, a real ladies' man, and Maggie wasn't about to become another notch on his bedpost.

"Thanks for coming," she said, trying to remember her manners as well as hide her surprise.

"I'm glad I could help out." He brushed a soft kiss on her cheek and gave her a hug. The scent of peppermint, leather and musk lingered long after he released her.

"How much do I owe you for the airline ticket?" Maggie asked.

"Don't worry about it." He placed a hand on her back and ushered her through the terminal. "This wing-ding must be a big deal."

"It is," she told him. But she doubted he really understood.

She'd worked hard to see the new pediatric ICU become a reality, as had Rhonda Martin, another pediatrician in her office. Tonight's formal event, *El Baile Elegante,* was a gala intended to thank donors and secure their ongoing financial support. Even though Maggie could no longer stand being in the same room with Rhonda, professionalism demanded she attend.

"There's got to be a hundred guys in this city who'd love to take you to that shindig. I still don't understand why you asked me."

"Because I want a real friend to accompany me, and there don't seem to be too many friendly faces in Boston anymore."

His expression sobered, and he paused before responding. "I'm not like the people you usually hobnob with, Maggie. And I hope you don't expect me to be."

She didn't. When they'd first become friends at Buckaroo Ranch, Jake had been a rebel, a James Dean on horseback. And Maggie had been a young Marian the Librarian. She doubted he'd changed much, if at all, which was all right with her. Jake had a way of making life seem simple and uncomplicated. And he'd had a way of making her smile when life seemed unbearable.

She slid him a quick glance. The skinny kid had sure filled out. And grown up.

They continued toward the exit, walking along with other travelers who'd made Boston their destination.

"I'm sorry about your divorce," he said, his soft Southern drawl washing over her like a warm summer rain. "Are you doing okay?"

Not really, but she was making progress. "My pride took a bigger hit than my heart, but I'll be all right."

Jake didn't comment, and she was grateful. Lord knew she'd psychoanalyzed herself enough in the past six months.

Learning that her husband Tom and Rhonda had conceived a baby had hurt, particularly since they hadn't waited until Maggie and Tom had officially separated to do so. Still, the split had been somewhat clean and amicable, but only because Maggie refused to make a scene or act as though Tom's affair had bothered her more than a broken nail.

She'd fought long and hard to become a professional, and that's the only behavior she expected from herself.

The voices from the past that sometimes nagged at her, jeered at her now, pointing out her shortcomings and hanging them out to dry.

What's wrong with you, Maggie? Stupid girl. Can't you do anything right?

She'd grown up with insufferable criticism. Her mother's third husband had been a drunk. *An alcoholic,* her clinical side corrected, although either diagnosis seemed to fit.

Oftentimes he'd said things that were cruel and untrue,

but Maggie had proven him wrong. The valedictorian at Valley View High had gone on to receive a full academic scholarship at Radcliffe, then transferred to Harvard Medical School, where she'd graduated number two in her class. Dr. Margaret Templeton wasn't stupid.

Or a failure.

And she hoped appearing at *El Baile Elegante* with Jake would show her colleagues that the failed marriage was merely a joint decision to end what wasn't working. Maggie Templeton, they would realize, was doing just fine without a husband.

She glanced to her side and found the handsome cowboy perusing her with a crooked grin and a glimmer in his eyes.

Jake couldn't help but admire the pretty doctor—in more ways than one. She'd achieved everything she'd set her mind to. And what's more, the quiet teenage girl he'd once called Magpie had grown up to be a real head-turner, the kind of lady a man couldn't help but notice.

Her hair, no longer the color of corn silk, had darkened to a golden blonde. And those caramel-colored eyes still held a tender heart, as well as a sadness few people could see.

Fifteen years ago, she'd been all knees and elbows, but she'd become womanly, with the kind of gentle curves a man liked to run his hands along all through the night.

"How are you, Magpie? Or should I call you doctor?"

"Just Maggie will do." She adjusted the shoulder strap of her purse. "I sure appreciate your coming out here like this."

For three long-ago summers, her grandma had shipped her off to Buckaroo Ranch, where Jake lived with his sister and tough-as-rawhide uncle. The sad-eyed bookworm had become the only friend he'd had growing up.

He gave her elbow a gentle squeeze. "I owe you one, remember?"

She'd protected him from a beating when he was sixteen by saying a nearly full bottle of Jack Daniel's had belonged to her. It hadn't, of course. Maggie had always been a moral crusader when it came to alcohol, unlike Jake who'd thought drinking and smoking made him more manly and grown-up.

Because she was a paying guest at the ranch, his uncle had merely poured the whiskey onto the dirt, then threatened to send her packing if it ever happened again. Uncle Dave wouldn't have been that easy on Jake.

And Jake hadn't had any other place to go home to.

"Are you talking about that bottle of Jack Daniel's?" she asked.

"My uncle would have given me the boot. He never did appreciate having to raise his brother's ornery son." Nor did he ever let Jake forget what a disappointment he was.

"You did have a rebellious streak, Jake."

"Still do."

She laughed. "I don't doubt it. But your uncle wasn't that bad. He never gave your sister a hard time."

"Sharon was a straight-A student. Like you, Magpie."

"Maybe you should have tried harder."

"Maybe so, but I never liked school." *Any of them.* He'd lost count of all the schools he'd attended in the early years. So by the time he was old enough to ride a bike, he began playing hooky every chance he got. Folks just thought he was a truant and a troublemaker, but Jake saw it as a means of self-preservation.

Chasing away the painful memories, he focused on Maggie. At one time, he'd actually had a crush on her, a sort of younger guy-older woman thing. He doubted that she'd ever picked up on it, though, since he'd been shy around girls back then.

He wasn't shy anymore.

Of course, he didn't allow women to get close enough to figure out what a good actor he was, or how he skated around the truth and kept them at a safe distance.

"You know," Maggie said, "I was really sorry to hear about Sharon's death."

"Me, too." Jake had loved his sister and would miss her. She'd been the only family he had left, and her death had been a senseless blow.

But in addition to grief, Sharon's death had also saddled Jake with the dude ranch he'd always hated and thrust him into instant parenthood, something he knew nothing about. As much as he loved Kayla and Sam, he was still uneasy around his niece and nephew, still worried that he'd screw up something important in their lives.

Maggie stepped onto the escalator and turned to face him, as he got in line behind her. Their eyes met, and he caught a whiff of her floral scent. Something purple. Lilacs, he guessed. "Let's talk about California."

She shrugged. "There's not much to tell. After this weekend, I'm going to tie up some loose ends, then move my practice."

He'd always been the kind to skip out on problems, not Maggie. But Jake was the last one in the world to say anything about leaving old memories behind. "How much time do we have before this hoopla?"

"Just enough time to go home and change clothes."

Twenty minutes later, Maggie unlocked the door and let Jake into her home—a small, renovated apartment she'd temporarily moved into. The place was clean, with white walls and shell-colored carpet.

Another woman might have hung a brightly colored,

artsy print on the wall, put a vase of flowers on the barren fireplace mantel, but Maggie hadn't gone to the trouble.

What did it matter? She'd be moving to the West Coast soon and had no reason to decorate or entertain anyone.

Jake glanced at the stark white walls. "Nice place you have."

"I suppose it needs a bit of color," she said, wishing she'd put a little more effort into decorating.

"I'm used to motels. If the place is clean, all I need is a soft bed and somewhere to hang my hat."

A bed. And a place to hang his hat.

Maggie's senses tingled, and she struggled to recognize a bit of the teenage boy she used to know. She saw only brief glimpses.

Who was this man who would spend the weekend with her?

This is Jake, she reminded herself. Some things didn't change. "Come on in. I'll show you the guest room."

Boots clicked upon the hardwood floors, chasing an odd sense of masculine presence over her like angel fingers strumming across harp strings.

She led him to the spare room down the hall, and as he dropped his bag on the guest bed, a flood of sexual awareness washed over her. Where had the short, gangly teenager gone?

"I'm wearing what I have on," he said.

Her eyes swept over him again. Cowboy boots, denim pants and a suede jacket were a far cry from what the other men would be wearing, but on Jake they looked great.

He reached into his tote bag and removed a black bolo. "This is as black-tie as I get."

She didn't doubt that for a minute. If he didn't mind walking into a formal affair dressed like a rebellious cowboy, she wouldn't complain. She actually fancied herself on his arm. "You look fine to me."

"I'm glad." He slid her a lazy smile, one that made her pulse zip and skip like the stones he'd taught her how to skim across the surface of the old swimming hole.

"Well," she said, "I'd better get dressed. If you'll excuse me, I won't be long."

But getting dressed took much longer than she'd anticipated.

She'd wanted to look her best because *El Baile Elegante* was a big event, one all of her colleagues would be attending. An event at which she believed they would be watching her, checking to see if her professional demeanor would falter when Tom and Rhonda entered the banquet hall. Of course, she was nervous.

But for some reason, knowing that Jake was in the living room, waiting to escort her to the gala, had her nerves even more on edge. Jumpy. The butterflies in her stomach had grown to an angry swarm.

She fidgeted with her hair for ten minutes, trying to sweep it up in an elegant coiffure, but the silky strands wouldn't stay put. She finally gave up and let it fall naturally to her shoulders. And even though she'd been putting on lipstick for years, her hands trembled and she had to reapply the lip liner three times before she was reasonably satisfied.

Maggie stood before the bathroom mirror and sighed. She'd done the best she could, under the circumstances. Now, if she could just hurry the evening along, get it over with and go back home, she'd be okay.

She entered the living room wearing a formal-length, black gown, with a scooped neckline in front. The other side plunged, revealing a V-shaped glimpse of her back. She had a strange urge to run down the hall and grab a wrap, something with which to cover herself, but it had been an unseasonably hot September day, and the evening promised to be humid and warm.

"Definitely worth the wait," Jake said. His appreciative grin complimented her in a way Tom never had. It both pleased and unnerved her further.

"Thank you."

As she fingered the strapless purse in her hands, his gaze locked on to hers. "What kind of fool would leave you?"

A part of her desperately needed to believe her ex had been a fool. "Tom Bradley, stockbroker extraordinaire."

"Remind me never to let him invest any of my money."

She smiled, grateful for the support, but too rational to believe she hadn't erred, that she hadn't somehow been at fault. She should have seen it coming, should have done something to prevent it. "I'm sure part of the blame was mine."

"What part?"

"I don't know," she said with a sigh. "My mom couldn't seem to make a marriage work. I didn't have much of an example."

"What about TV reruns?" he asked, stepping closer. "Ward and June had a heck of a marriage."

Maggie laughed. That's what she liked about Jake. He had a way of making her troubles vanish, like he had all those years ago when they'd slipped away from the ranch and gone fishing in the creek. Or when they'd sneaked out late at night and gone for a hike.

She'd missed him, his fun-loving spirit and easy smile. "You're right. The Cleavers had a perfect relationship. Now I realize what I did wrong."

He grinned in that cocky way of his, only this time

more grown-up, more provocative. "What did you do wrong?"

"I didn't do the dishes while wearing pearls, a dress and heels."

"Maybe you should have skipped the dress and just worn the heels and pearls. It would have made me come home."

She swatted his arm and countered with a playful smile. "There's more to a relationship than sex."

"My best relationships have been based on great sex. What else is there?"

"Kids and picket fences."

Jake slowly shook his head. "Babies are scary."

"Not to Tom. About two years ago he started asking me about having a child. I wasn't ready then. Children have very important needs, and a doctor who's still paying off student loans doesn't have time to spend stay-at-home, quality time with them." She blew out a ragged breath. "Now, Rhonda Martin, another pediatrician in my office, is expecting his child."

"So," Jake said, settling into a more serious tone. "What are you going to do when this evening is over? Rhonda will still be expecting a baby, and you and Tom will still be divorced."

Maggie unsnapped her purse and withdrew the car keys. "I'm going to start packing boxes for my move to California. A friend from medical school referred me to a respected pediatrician in Los Angeles who is retiring. I'm going to take over his practice."

"Atta girl." Jake chuckled. "Moving on has always worked for me."

"That's the way I see it, too," she said, heading toward the front door. "I'll be leaving day after tomorrow, even though I don't start work for two more months."

"Why so soon?"

"Because Rhonda and I work together and maintain a cordial business relationship at the office. For some reason, people feel inclined to invite me to share in the celebrations, parties and good wishes. And the truth is, I can't stand the thought of receiving another invitation to a baby shower, even though I politely decline each one."

He cocked his head and furrowed his brow. "You're being treated as a lifelong friend of the bride and groom?"

"I guess it's my own fault for acting as though I didn't care." She sighed heavily. "It seemed like the professionally correct thing to do, when what I really wanted to do was jerk her by the stethoscope around her neck and give her a piece of my mind."

"So you pretended it didn't bother you?" He took her hand and gave it a slow, gentle squeeze. Her fingers warmed at his touch, her heart at his compassion. "You still have to be perfect, don't you, Magpie?"

"I try to be the best I can be," she said. "I don't consider it a personal flaw or shortcoming."

Jake grinned and shook his head. "Honey, I doubt a word or two from me is going to change anything."

She appreciated the fact that he didn't preach or patronize her. "Hard work and dedication are important to me."

"I know." Jake ran the knuckles of his hand along her cheek, sending a swirl of heat to her face, and no doubt, causing a blush to surface. "So what's my role tonight?"

"Your role?" She didn't mean to throw the question back in his lap, but she wasn't sure what she expected, other than a friend to hold her hand. Maybe ask her to dance. "I don't really know."

"You want me to be an old friend? A new friend? A

guy you've been dating?'' He slid her a cocky, James Dean smile. ''Your lover?''

She shook her head and laughed. ''At first I'd just wanted an escort, a friend. Someone to lean on for my last hurrah.''

''And now?'' he asked, blue eyes studying her intently. His musky scent closed in on her, sharpening her senses, making her keenly aware of his masculinity. A lot had happened to them in fifteen years. And at this very moment, she realized Jake had developed a sensuality he'd never had as a lanky teenager.

''You could act as though we're dating, I suppose.''

''Have we made love?'' His question startled her, excited her.

She gazed at him, unable to prevent her thoughts from drifting to Jake, lying in her bed, sheets draped low across his hips. Oh, for Pete's sake. Her imagination had never taken sexual turns before tonight. ''Of course not.''

''But we want to, right?''

Her heart zinged and pinged, and a heat settled low in her stomach. Make love to Jake? The vision of a naked cowboy in her bed hit her full force, and she struggled to regain control of her thoughts. He was role-playing and getting his act straight, and she was allowing her libido to interfere. ''Well…''

''Okay,'' he said. ''I get it. We've kissed a time or two. And I want to kiss you again and see what flavor of breath mints you use. I want to hold you in my arms again, sway to a slow love song, feel your breasts against my chest. And I have a hankering to see how far things will go tonight. After the gala.''

For some reason, she felt as if she were in the midst of phone sex. His slow, Southern drawl poured over her, making her want to take an active role in his game. "I'd like people to think I'm happy and glad to be single."

"We'll make them wonder what we've got planned for later on."

"I didn't mean for this to be a chore," she said, having second thoughts about role-playing with a man who made her mind drift to the bedroom. She'd been sleeping single in a king-size bed for too darn long, not that she had any inclination to change that. "If you just want to be my escort for the evening, it's okay. In fact, that's probably best."

"Hey, I don't mind helping out. That's what friends are for."

She clutched her purse against her heart and offered the handsome cowboy a shy smile. "I've never been too good at acting."

He stepped behind her and placed a calloused hand on her lower back. The touch of his work-roughened palm and splayed fingers against her skin sent a jolt of heat to her core, and she had the strangest desire to feel those hands on her entire body.

"Let me do the acting," he said. "Just follow my lead."

"I'm not sure I can pull this off, Jake. Maybe we should just be friends."

He opened the door for her. "Trust me, Magpie. It'll be easy. You'll see."

She hoped his words rang true, but something told her this was going to be a wild, unpredictable evening.

And she didn't know if that made her feel better or worse.

Chapter Two

Crystal chandeliers cast an elegant glow inside the New England Garden Towers, as Jake ushered Maggie down the carpeted hallway to the Grand Ballroom. He would make it through the evening without a scratch, but he wasn't so sure about Maggie.

"I'm nervous," she whispered.

"I know." He took her trembling hand and placed it in the crook of his arm, his fingers covering hers, offering his support, his strength.

He wanted to chase her fears away, be some kind of superhero who would make everything be all right. He'd tried to do the same thing when they were kids, but it had been easier when Maggie had been a shy, studious sixteen-year-old, and he'd been a surly teen who resented the life fate had dealt him.

During those three summers they'd spent together, he'd taken her hand more times than he could remember. And he'd taught her how to loosen up and have fun, at least for a few months out of the year.

One afternoon, he'd come across her reading, alone in her room, and dragged her out to the pond. She'd been afraid to take the rope and swing across the lake the first time, but he'd wrapped his arms around her and swung with her, coaxing her to let go, to trust him.

"It's just like swinging over the swimming hole," he told her. "It wasn't nearly as scary as you thought."

"Well, this feels like I'm dangling over an alligator-infested swamp, rather than a small, secluded lake."

He didn't understand her nervousness. Maggie was a hell of a woman, and a man would be proud to have her as a friend or a lover.

In fact, if she weren't such a good friend and so vulnerable, he'd suggest that they continue the lover charade when he took her home, just for tonight. But Maggie deserved more than that. More than a one-night stand with a footloose cowboy who wasn't what he seemed.

He squeezed her hand. "I'm with you, darlin', and we'll make it through the evening without a hitch."

Just ahead, Jake spotted a table where a matronly woman wearing a black, beaded gown sat with gold lettered name tags and a guest list.

Maggie cleared her throat to speak. Jake sensed her nerves had settled in her voice, so he took the lead. "Dr. Margaret Templeton and Jake Meredith."

She glanced up at him, appreciation peeking from those soulful, brown eyes.

Maggie might have become a respected physician, but on the inside, she was still the same shy girl. He tilted her chin and gazed into her eyes. "You look beautiful, honey."

She whispered a "thank you," but he figured her appreciation went far beyond his compliment.

After slapping on his name tag, Jake placed a hand on the sway of Maggie's bare back and ushered her to the open doorway.

"I can hardly take my eyes off you," he said, letting his hand slip low on her hip in an intimate, possessive gesture.

She tilted her head, and honey-brown eyes sought his, looking, it seemed, for an indication of honesty. She would find it. Maggie was the most beautiful woman he'd ever had on his arm and certainly the most elegant. He wanted her to know it. Feel it.

Before they could step away from the doorway, a heavyset gentleman with gray at the temples strode toward them and gave Maggie a kiss on the cheek. She introduced Jake to Dr. George Walters, and the men shared the customary handshakes and greetings.

The doctor scanned Jake's formal Western wear. "You're not from around here, are you?"

"Nope. Texas, born and bred."

A waiter, balancing a full tray of flutes on his arm, cautiously approached. "Excuse me. Can I offer you some champagne?"

"Yes." Jake took a glass from the waiter, handed it to Maggie and snagged one for himself. A drink would take the edge off her nervousness, even if she hadn't changed her mind about the evils of alcohol. When they were teenagers, he'd been hell-bent to acquire a taste for whiskey, and she'd tried her best to reform him. To an extent, he supposed, she'd made her point.

He didn't drink for the heck of it, like his old man had done, but that didn't mean he didn't appreciate the taste of good bourbon or an ice-cold beer. He just kept a close count of how many he enjoyed.

Rather than taking a sip, Maggie held on to the long-stemmed flute as though needing something to keep her hands busy.

He lifted his glass and clinked it against hers. "Drink up, Magpie."

Dr. Walter lifted a gray peppery brow at either the suggestion or the nickname. "Have you two known each other long?"

"Fifteen years," Jake said. "And now that's she's free of Tom Bradley, I'm staking my claim."

His claim? Maggie nearly choked on the champagne, sending a shot of fizz up her nose.

Jake's blue eyes caught hers, and he gently touched her shoulder like a concerned suitor. "Are you all right, honey?"

She nodded. "Fine. I'm fine."

Would she be able to pull off this silly act? Jake seemed so natural, so good at playing his part, but she felt like a ballerina in combat boots.

"What line of work are you in?" George asked Jake.

Maggie hoped he was just trying to make polite, cocktail-hour small talk, but she had a feeling he was digging for more information about the man who was staking his claim on Tom Bradley's ex-wife.

"I'm a horse trainer."

"Thoroughbreds?"

"Nope. Rodeo horses."

"Jake owns a ranch and is one of the best horseman around," Maggie added. Sharon had raved about his ability to connect with animals, especially horses, once referring to him as Cowboy Doolittle. And Maggie had seen it herself, years ago. "He has an uncanny way with animals."

Dr. Walters nodded judiciously, and Maggie decided it was best they move on. "If you'll excuse us, George, I need to speak to someone."

"Certainly." The doctor extended a hand to Jake. "Perhaps, later you can tell me about your ranch."

"Maybe so." Jake placed an empty champagne glass upon a small table by the door, then slipped his hand low upon Maggie's back. His thumb caressed her skin, sending a swirl of heat to her spinal cord and then throughout her body.

Her reaction to his touch made it easier to play along and pretend they shared an intimacy known to lovers, which was a good thing, she supposed. But she didn't need to lose her head. She and Jake were friends, and that's all they would ever be. He was a Texan, through and through. And she was a dedicated physician, with a new practice waiting for her in California, a prosperous practice that would enable her to pay off the remainder of her student loans.

They mingled among the well-dressed crowd, greeted people and made polite conversation. All the while, Jake was charming and attentive. More than one woman cast a lingering gaze his way and smiled when she thought no one was looking. Jake, it seemed, caught every glance, every flirtatious smile, and sent them right back, all the while remaining attentive to Maggie. His gift, she realized, wasn't limited to animals.

Jake was an attractive man, not just in his rugged good looks, but in his manner, his demeanor. Maggie felt as though she'd snagged the gold ring on the dating merry-go-round, and she found herself proud to be with him, at least as long as the short ride lasted.

Several times, he took her half-empty champagne flute and replaced it with a full glass. A warmth had settled into her bones, and the entire evening became much easier to bear.

Until Tom and Rhonda walked into the room.

Maggie glanced toward the doorway and stiffened. "They're here," she whispered.

"I was just beginning to think the evening was going to be a slam dunk." Jake glanced at the doorway. "Let's go say hello, then we can put it behind us, Magpie."

"I guess you're right."

He flashed her a crooked smile and cupped her cheek. "You're in good hands, darlin'. We'll make it nice and sweet, then the worst will be over."

Just like he'd been able to do years before, Jake had a way of cutting to the chase, of helping her face her demons. Of being the kind of friend she needed at any given time. "You're right. Let's do it."

She took a step forward, but he pulled her back, accosting her with a woodsy scent of musk and something else. Something she could only describe as essence of cowboy. She breathed deep, relishing his presence, his strength.

Tilting her chin with the tip of his finger, he bent his head to brush his lips upon her partially opened mouth. Once, twice. It was just a whisper of a kiss, soft and sweet, but so sensually delightful, that she closed her eyes and was swept away from the crowd and onto some hidden stage far from the reality of the gala. She doubted whether she could have been more moved by an openmouthed prelude to foreplay.

In fact, she wanted to grab him by the suede lapels and pull him closer, deepen the kiss, see where it might take them both. But she didn't. Her staunch professionalism wouldn't allow it.

When she opened her eyes, he flashed her a cocky, bad-boy smile. "How was that for suggesting we're more than friends?"

Suggesting? Friends didn't kiss like that, and even though she knew better, that slow, sensuous contact had nearly convinced her that they'd always been more than friends. Which, of course, they hadn't. So why had his kiss nearly sent her to the moon? She tried to regain her footing. "That was some kiss."

"You have a mouth made for kissing. All kinds of kisses, short and sweet, long and deep."

At the thought of kissing Jake thoroughly, her knees nearly buckled, and heat pooled low in her belly. She quickly struggled to recover.

Jake had been a bachelor for years, and from what his sister had said, women clamored around him. He had kissing down to a science and was, undoubtedly, a master at the fine art of seduction. So he'd been able to pack something powerful into that whisper of a kiss, all for the sake of the roles they were playing.

"Come on, let's get this over with," she said, leading him toward the middle of the room where Tom and Rhonda conversed with a waiter bearing a tray of champagne.

She assessed her ex-husband in a way she never had before and found him lacking in more ways than one. He stood several inches shorter than Jake and appeared pale and wan next to the Texan's sun-bronzed complexion. Funny, but she'd never noticed what the indoor lighting had done to his skin. "Hello, Tom. Rhonda. It's good to see you."

Tom smiled, and for the very first time, she noticed his

thin lips. Like a turkey's beak. No wonder his kisses had never sent her heart spinning. He'd been shortchanged in the lip-and-mouth department, so it seemed. "How have you been, Maggie?"

"Great." She tried to muster a sense of pride, then turned to Jake, whose full lips curled in that James Dean grin. "I'd like you to meet a friend of mine, Jake Meredith."

The men greeted each other, and when Tom introduced Rhonda, Jake flashed her a charming smile, working his magic, it seemed, on the pregnant pediatrician. "Pleased to meet you, ma'am."

"Thank you." Rhonda smiled and cast an admiring gaze on the sexy cowboy.

"Rhonda isn't feeling well," Tom said, slipping an arm around his wife. "So we'll probably only stay for dinner."

"That's too bad." Maggie couldn't conjure the least bit of sympathy. She actually hoped the woman's feet swelled to the size of a full-grown elephant's, and that her back ached like crazy. "The ninth month can be unpleasant."

"Yes, but it's also exciting," Rhonda said. "We have the nursery all ready. You'll have to come by and see it."

Oh gosh, not again. Did Rhonda's whole world revolve around Tom and the baby? Or was she purposely waving a victory flag in Maggie's face?

Well, she could have Turkey-lips. And his baby. A man who cheated on his wife wasn't a prize, as far as Maggie was concerned.

"Better you, Rhonda, than me," Maggie said, referring to Rhonda's husband, not her pregnancy.

"Some women aren't meant to be mothers," Rhonda said.

Maggie wished the pediatrician was wearing a stethoscope so Maggie could wrap it tight around the woman's throat and choke her until she turned blue. The pregnant glow was hard enough to tolerate; the pregnant gloat was pushing Maggie's professional resolve to the limit.

"Hey," Jake said, taking Maggie's hand and tilting his head toward the waiters bringing in trays laden with dinner plates. "I think they want us to take our seats."

Maggie quickly nodded, ready to escape the upcoming discussion of cribs and wallpaper.

"You're a lifesaver," she whispered to Jake. "And quite the charmer. I think Rhonda found you attractive."

"Maybe so," he said, sliding her a slow smile. "There's something women love about cowboys."

Yes, Maggie supposed there was. Particularly, a cowboy like Jake.

"But I've got a hell of a lot better cull shoot than Tom Bradley," he said, pulling her close to his side. "I know which fillies to keep and which to let go. Come on, Magpie. Let's find us a quiet place to sit."

They stayed only for dinner and a dance, long enough to make a gracious showing, then Maggie and Jake left and drove home.

As they strode across her parking garage toward the elevator, Maggie winced. She should have opted for the expensive black heels, rather than the fashionable strappy sandals she'd purchased to go with her evening dress. While they waited for the door to open, she curled her toes, trying to eliminate the pain her new shoes had caused.

"What's the matter?" Jake asked.

The fact that he'd picked up on her discomfort surprised her, but in the past, he'd always been in tune with her feelings. Apparently, he was just as discerning now. How was that possible?

Tom had always been too wrapped up in himself to give much notice to Maggie. In the evenings, he'd always asked for a head-and-neck rub, stating how stressful his day had been. Maggie'd had plenty of stressful days, but she'd never asked for any special attention.

"Just an uncomfortable pair of shoes," she said, not wanting to complain. "It's no big deal."

They rode the elevator up to the fifth floor, and she led the way to the little apartment she called a temporary home.

Jake took the key from her hand and unlocked the door. "Go inside and make yourself comfortable."

She'd intended to, but his suggestion took her aback. It had a slight, seductive sound to it. Or maybe he was just being nice, and her imagination had read seduction into his words.

This was Jake, her old friend, she again reminded herself. But the ex-rodeo star had, according to his sister, acquired more than his share of gold buckles along with a host of female fans eager to join his fan club.

Loyal childhood friend or sexy ladies' man? She tried to reconcile the two images, but found it difficult.

"Take off your shoes," he said, his voice intoxicatingly smooth, like a velvety shot of whiskey.

"I beg your pardon?"

"I'm going to give you a foot massage." He bolted the door, which gave her an odd, anticipatory sensation, one that was sexually charged, at least on her part. Surely, he didn't mean to seduce her, because she wasn't sure how much of a struggle she'd put up. And a one-night stand with an old friend would certainly complicate her life.

"You don't have to do that. I'll be all right, once I get

out of these shoes.'' She dropped her purse onto one of the barstools that faced the mirrored bar in the living room, then removed the sandals that had blistered her feet and placed them in the seat, next to her evening bag. ''I'll be fine as soon as I can run around barefoot.''

Jake slipped off his suede jacket and draped it over the sofa. Then he removed his bolo tie and undid the top buttons on his shirt, revealing a dark patch of chest hair. She really shouldn't stand there and stare at him, but she couldn't remember when she'd last watched a man undress and found it so interesting, so arousing. So tempting.

He strode toward the living-room window and gazed out at the brightly lit Boston skyline. Her interest followed his. Stars glittered in the sky, offering a magical ambiance that she'd never known the plain apartment had.

''It's a pretty view,'' he said, ''if you like big city sights.''

''You're right.'' Maggie studied the evening panorama, amazed that she hadn't noticed it before.

He turned slowly, then his gaze swept over her, lingering, it seemed, upon her face. She brushed a strand of hair from her cheek. What did he see? What was so interesting?

She cleared her throat. ''Would you like to have something to drink? Coffee? An after-dinner liqueur?''

He studied her as though the offer had surprised him. She wasn't sure why. It seemed a friendly thing to suggest, even though she'd already drank more this evening than she had the past year.

''I guess you finally acquired a taste for alcohol,'' he said.

''Not really. I enjoy an occasional glass of wine.''

''And champagne,'' he said with a lazy smile.

''Only when someone fills my glass.'' She nodded toward the mirrored bar that graced the sunken living room. "The liquor belonged to Tom, but he left it behind when he moved out. He and Rhonda are on a health kick, so he says. I'll probably pour it all out rather than pack it all up and move it again."

He nodded sagely, as though he understood much more than she'd told him. He'd always had an amazing ability to read a person, to reach under the surface. She wondered what he saw in her.

"How about a glass of wine?" he asked. "I've never been partial to fancy liqueurs."

"Sure. I hope you like a dry white. It's all I have."

She started toward the kitchen, but he strode forward and placed a hand upon her shoulder to still her steps. "Don't bother, Maggie. I'll get it. Just take a seat in the easy chair."

He'd already reached the kitchen and had begun opening the cupboards before she could argue.

"Wineglasses are in the dining-room hutch," she said. "And a bottle is chilling in the fridge."

In no time at all, he'd prepared two drinks, then brought one to her. He nodded toward the chintz-covered easy chair and matching ottoman. "Now, sit down and put your feet up."

She should have declined, but for some reason, a foot massage sounded incredibly nice. And luxurious. She padded across the room and took a seat, sinking into the softness of the chair Tom hadn't liked.

Jake handed her a glass of wine, then straddled the ottoman. His knees corralled her feet. "Do you have any lotion?"

Kama Sutra oil came to mind, but she quickly whisked the naughty thought away. If she wasn't careful, she'd embarrass them both with some crazy suggestion that would screw up a perfectly good friendship. No pun intended.

Good grief, she'd thought about sex more this evening than she had in the past year. What was it about Jake that made her mind stray in a sexual direction? Was it because the sensual cowboy knew how to treat a lady? Or was it her own fascination and curiosity?

"You have pretty feet. They're soft and smooth. I like the polish."

"I just had a pedicure," she said, as though needing an explanation. "Because of the strappy sandals."

"I hope you tipped her well. She did a great job."

As he kneaded her foot, she found herself slipping back into the softness of the chair. She closed her eyes, relishing each deft movement of his fingers, his thumbs. And suddenly she wanted his hands to continue up her leg. The massage, at least in her mind, had turned into a sensual rub. And if it hadn't felt so darn good, she would have told him to stop.

Jake watched Maggie slowly unwind and relax; the foot rub had helped. He'd given his share of massages in the past, with other women and usually as an act of foreplay. He'd offered one to Maggie as a token of friendship, not as a means to get her into bed. But it had a strange effect on him. He wanted to stroke her calf, work his way to her knee, along the inside of her thigh. Coax her into a state of arousal.

Her eyes opened, and she grazed him with a heated glance, one that told him she, too, was finding the massage far more stimulating than either of them had intended. Had she been any other woman, Jake would have known exactly what to do, what to say. But with Maggie, the words stuck in his throat.

He placed her foot on the ottoman, then picked up the

other and continued to work. He'd hoped changing feet, and not progressing up her leg would ease the powerful urge he had to take her in his arms, to carry her to bed. But it hadn't.

"You're incredible," she said.

He thought she meant his hands, but her eyes told another story, one he wasn't prepared to pursue. Not if he wanted to wake up in the morning without any regrets.

Shoot, not that he'd regret making love to Maggie. But she was the one he was worried about, the one who'd been hurt, the one who needed time to mend. And Jake was the last guy in the world who could help her. She deserved more than a one-night stand, and that's about all he could offer her.

"Thanks," he said. "I've had a lot of practice."

She lifted a brow, as though his experience bothered her. "Sharon said you had a slew of women chasing after you."

He shrugged. "I've never made any promises about love and forever, but that doesn't seem to keep women from wanting to change my attitude and my lifestyle."

"And you have no intention of doing that?"

"I'm honest with the women I date. I'm not the marrying kind, but I do believe in one-on-one relationships until they don't work anymore."

"I guess having a family has curtailed your love life."

Talking to Maggie about sex, or the lack of it, seemed strange. "I intend to provide those kids with the best home and family I can, even if it means hiring the right people to give it to them. And I'm not about to drag a 'slew of women' through their life. If that means a steady diet of celibacy, then I guess that's what'll happen."

"You'll be a good dad for them."

"I don't think so, but I'm going to try."

Jake's cell phone rang, interrupting the conversation he hadn't wanted to continue. As he pulled the phone from the clip on his belt, apprehension dropped like a rock in the pit of his stomach. He hoped it wasn't Rosa calling. His biggest fear was that something would happen to the kids he was supposed to protect.

Glancing at the lit display, he recognized the number and swallowed hard. It *was* Rosa, and she wouldn't call unless it was an emergency.

Had Sam taken another tumble and cracked his noggin? The last one had blackened his little eye and required stitches.

Did Kayla have another fever? About a month ago, she ran a high temperature and lay around the house like a rag doll. Just a virus, the doctor had said, but the whole experience had scared Jake senseless.

He couldn't eat or sleep when the kids were hurt or sick. Things like that hit him hard. He just wanted them to stay happy and healthy.

"Hello, Rosa."

"It's not Rosa, Jake. It's her daughter, Sara."

Panic backhanded him. Why couldn't Rosa talk? Were Sam and Kayla okay? "What's wrong?"

"The kids are fine," Sara said. "But my mother is in the hospital and in a great deal of pain. The doctor said it's her gall bladder and that she needs surgery. When can you come home?"

"I'll try to fly standby first thing in the morning." Jake glanced at Maggie, who sat attentively, her eyes intensely watching him. "Can you stay with the kids until I get home?"

Sara agreed, but asked him to hurry since she had to return to school on Monday morning.

When he hung up the phone, Maggie squeezed his hand. "What's the matter?"

"Rosa needs to have surgery. I've got to get home."

"Are the kids okay?"

"Yeah, Sara, her college-aged daughter, is with them."

"Well, that's good."

Was it? That's not the way he saw it. As long as Kayla and Sam were with someone other than Jake, they were fine. But what would happen when the poor kids had to depend on him to look after them? The thought of being more than a visiting uncle scared the devil out of him. What did he know about being a father? It's not like he'd ever had a decent role model.

"Jake," Maggie said. "You're pale. Is there something you're not telling me?"

He looked at her, unsure of how much he wanted to admit and deciding not too much. "I don't know anything about kids. How am I going to take care of them without Rosa?"

"Hire someone."

"Who?" he asked, unsure of who he could trust or depend on to do right by the kids.

"How about Rosa's daughter?"

"Sara has to go back to Rice University on Monday morning. She's got a test or something."

"I could come and help with the kids," she said, "at least for a month or so."

"I'll be okay," he said, hoping he could convince her, even if he couldn't convince himself. He glanced at the phone in the kitchen. Maybe he should call the airline and find an early-morning flight back to Texas.

"Why don't you let me come help?"

He shook his head. "I can't ask you to do that."

"Why not? You need help. I'm available for about six

weeks, just long enough for Rosa to recover from her surgery.''

Her offer was appealing, even though he was hesitant to risk having her find out he wasn't good at dealing with kids, that Kayla was angry at him most of the time. Still, he needed help. And he wasn't sure where to find someone he could trust.

Shoot, having a doctor to watch over Kayla and Sam would be a godsend. They'd never get hurt or sick. Or if they did, she'd cure them in a heartbeat. Pride battled his desire to see the kids in good hands.

His reluctance to accept her help still hovered around him. ''Are you sure you don't mind?''

''I owe you one, now.'' A smile dimpled her cheeks, and her caramel-brown eyes glimmered. ''I was dreading this evening more than you'll ever know, and you helped me through it.'' She stood. ''I can't fly to Texas with you, because I have some things to take care of first. I'll have to get the moving and storage people to come earlier than I'd planned.''

''And you'll need to pour out all that liquor,'' he said.

She smiled. ''That, too. And besides, I'm going to drive. I'll need my car in California.''

He swallowed hard. How long would he be alone with the kids? An hour sometimes seemed like forever. Could he manage without help for a day or two? ''When do you think you'll arrive?''

''By Thursday or Friday. Will that be all right?''

''Sure.'' It would have to be. ''No problem.''

Had he really agreed to have her come and help? To move in with him and the kids for a month or so? To be in such close proximity that she'd see how useless he was as a father? To have her learn that his cavalier attitude masked his shortcomings? He'd always made it a point not to let women get close enough to see his flaws, to find him lacking.

She pulled her foot from his hand, offering him a glimpse of her bare inner leg, the inside of her thigh that he'd wanted to touch, to stroke. Desire stirred, and he shifted his legs so she wouldn't know.

But *he* knew, and it brought about a whole new worry.

He hadn't had sex since he'd moved in with the kids. How was he going to handle the sexual attraction he felt, if she came to stay for a month or so?

Keeping a woman at a distance was hard to do once she'd shared a man's bed. There was no way he could let himself get involved with Dr. Maggie Templeton. Not sexually.

She stood. "Why don't I show you to the guest room. Since you need to wake up early, you'll probably want to get some sleep."

He nodded, although he wouldn't be able to sleep a wink tonight.

Or any of the nights to follow.

Chapter Three

Maggie turned off the highway at Winchester, the small Texas town that neighbored Buckaroo Ranch.

Winchester hadn't changed much in fifteen years. A streetlight had been erected on the corner of Main and Second, and Roy's Grocery was now the Main Street Market. Other than that, everything looked much the same.

She turned right at Avery's Feed Store and followed the old county road south, passing cattle grazing in green pastures. She and her stepfather had driven along this same road many times, and he never failed to complain about the money her paternal grandmother had paid for Maggie's summers at Buckaroo Ranch.

Why doesn't that old lady just give us the cash? You'd rather stay cooped up in your bedroom reading, anyway. Sending a lazy kid like you to a fancy camp is a waste of money.

Maggie had never responded to her stepdad's tirades,

mostly because he wouldn't have put up with her arguments, but also because there was more to her grandmother's offer than he knew.

Crippling arthritis had confined Gram to a convalescent home at the age of sixty-three, so the only escape from a dysfunctional home she could offer her granddaughter was three summers at Buckaroo Ranch.

The last, five-mile stretch passed quickly, and Maggie soon drove under the Ponderosa-style signpost that bore the name of the posh dude ranch Jake now owned.

Since this wasn't Sunday, the beginning of a Buckaroo week, there was no sign of the buckboards that carried guests and luggage from the parking lot to the plush cabins in which they would reside.

In the past, Rascal, the one-eyed cattle dog, had run beside the wagons, greeting those arriving with a bark and a wag of his stumpy tail, but he'd been an old dog then. With Sharon gone and Jake undoubtedly busy with the responsibilities that were now his, there wouldn't be a familiar face to welcome her to Buckaroo Ranch.

A pang of disappointment struck. As much as Maggie hated to admit it, she'd thought a lot about Jake in the past few days. Too much, in fact. She'd close her eyes and see the flirtatious glimmer in those intense blue eyes, feel the heat of his touch, relive the knee-weakening kiss.

She blew out a heavy sigh. She'd had enough psychology to know that her ex-husband's rejection had triggered a need to feel loved and worthy again. The attraction she felt for the grown-up Jake was entirely out of line, and the sooner she got the sexually charged thoughts under control, the better.

Instead of freshening up after six hours on the road, she gave only a cursory glance in the rearview mirror. She and Jake were old friends, for goodness' sake. There was no reason to primp.

Maggie grabbed her suitcase from the back seat, slipped the strap of her tote bag over a shoulder and shut the car door. She followed the shadow-dappled pathway that led to the house. Several of the outbuildings lay ahead—the hair salon and spa for those wanting more of a luxury vacation, the dining room where guests ate gourmet food while seated family style at long, wooden tables.

Nearing the house, she spotted an older man dressed in cowboy garb leading a mounted group along the riding trail that bordered the indoor arena. He looked a bit like Earl Iverson, the man who'd managed the ranch fifteen years ago, although grayer and much heavier.

She climbed the steps to the rustic front porch of Buckaroo Ranch, feeling as though she'd stepped into a time warp of *Twilight Zone* proportions. Everything seemed the same, yet eerily different.

For a moment, some of the old childhood insecurities crept back into the forefront of her mind.

Get a grip, she told herself. The gangly teen who had once perched awkwardly between woman and child no longer existed.

She lifted her hand to knock, but before her knuckles could rap on the carved-oak entry, the door swung open.

"Thank God, you're here." Jake took her bags, dropped them onto the floor and quickly swept her into his arms, accosting her with his scent of leather and musk.

Her heart did a swan dive, and her knees nearly gave out. But before she could react or speak, he grabbed her hand and pulled her into the house.

They crossed the Spanish-tiled entry, the leather soles of his boots clicking, her tennis shoes squeaking. Maggie briefly scanned the spacious living room, where the adult guests of old had always gathered for the cocktail hour. Other than a new cream-colored sectional in the corner and a few toys scattered on the floor, the room looked the same.

When Jake led her into the kitchen, she couldn't help but gasp.

A cyclone, it appeared, had swept through, causing major damage to the kitchen. Dirty dishes lined the counters and filled the sink, and splatters of food littered the walls and floor.

A towheaded toddler sat in a high chair, chocolate ice cream smeared across the tray like finger paint. The boy smiled in greeting, screeching and raising his spoon in a sticky fist.

"That's Sam," Jake said, nodding toward the messy little boy.

Sam offered a chocolaty smile, and Maggie couldn't help but grin. Had she ever enjoyed ice cream with such barbaric abandon?

"And this is Kayla," he added.

A little redheaded girl sat at the kitchen table, an open coloring book before her. She wore her curly hair loose and parted at the side, a red-and-black ladybug hair clip holding a large lock away from her face. Kermit-green eyes gazed at Maggie with wisdom beyond the little girl's years. All signs of the mild to moderate cerebral palsy that plagued Kayla appeared to lay dormant.

Five years ago, shortly after Kayla's birth, the pediatrician's diagnosis had rattled Sharon. Maggie had offered as much long-distance counseling as she could, before referring her friend to national support groups and online resources.

Extending a hand to Sharon's daughter, Maggie smiled warmly. "I'm glad to meet you, Kayla."

The little girl accepted the greeting, but continued to peruse the adult she'd been introduced to.

Such a solemn expression for a pretty little girl. Maggie wanted to put the child at ease. "Kayla, you look a lot like your mother."

Mentioning Sharon worked. The little girl smiled. "Thank you. Did you know my mommy?"

"I sure did. We were friends when we were kids."

"Kayla," Jake said. "This is Dr. Templeton. She's the one I was telling you about."

The girl, a pink crayon held in one hand like a scepter, furrowed an auburn brow. "You're a doctor?"

Maggie, who'd worked hard to earn the distinguished title, didn't expect friends to refer to her as such. "Why don't you just call me Maggie?"

"Do you give shots?" Crayon still raised and brow still furrowed, the little girl nibbled on her bottom lip while awaiting Maggie's reply.

"Only when absolutely necessary, but remember, I came to visit as a friend, not as a doctor."

"Maggie's going to help us until Rosa gets better," Jake explained.

The task suddenly looked a bit overwhelming, and Maggie couldn't help but scan the room again. Hadn't he been cleaning up after each meal?

Her eyes settled on the chocolate-covered toddler in the high chair. She'd always encouraged parents to let children feed themselves, but she now wondered whether chocolate ice cream should be an exception.

Jake leaned against the counter, next to the sinkful of dirty dishes, and crossed his arms. He looked windblown, tussled. And too damn sexy for his own good. Her heart did a little flip-flop, and she had to remind herself of her resolve to keep things on a platonic keel.

"Boy, am I glad you came," he said.

"I'll bet you are. You definitely need reinforcements." Maggie tucked a strand of hair behind her ear and surveyed the kitchen again. "Should we draw straws to decide who's going to tackle the cleanup?"

"We don't have to decide that yet. I've still got some dishes left in the cupboard." He laughed, then blew out a deep breath and nodded toward Sam. "I'm more concerned about cleaning up the little piglet. Would you mind helping?"

The poor kid was covered from the tips of his downy fine hair to the mismatched socks he wore. Apparently, Uncle Jake hadn't taken time to put on his shoes. Or maybe they'd been lost in the clutter.

"What would you have done if I hadn't arrived?" she asked.

He shot her one of those bad-boy grins. "Taken him out back and hosed him off, I guess."

Maggie lifted a brow and scrutinized her handsome cowboy friend. "Are you kidding? You haven't been hosing him down in the yard, have you?"

"No." He laughed again. "I was joking, Maggie. Actually, I've been filling the tub with warm, soapy water and swishing him around."

Uncle Jake was undoubtedly out of his element. The past few days must have been comical, and Maggie wished she could have witnessed them firsthand.

"Doctor," Kayla said, her voice far more serious than that of her uncle. "Do you read stories to kids?"

Maggie smiled at the girl. "I haven't had too many opportunities, but if you have some storybooks, I'd be happy to read to you."

"Goodie," Kayla said. "Because uncles don't like to read." Kayla shot an exasperated look at Jake, and Maggie realized it had been a bone of contention between the two.

She could certainly understand Kayla's frustration. Kids loved to listen to stories. Parents who didn't read to their children did them a huge disservice. Maybe she would have to work on Jake. Some people didn't believe an old dog could learn new tricks, but she disagreed.

"I'll just have to talk your uncle into reading you a story once in a while." She slid him a sly smile.

And Jake did his damnedest to return a grin, even though he wanted to scoff and stomp outside. Kayla was always grumpy when he refused to read aloud.

"Reading to children is good for them," Maggie added. "It helps them develop learning skills, not to mention a love of books."

Jake didn't doubt that for a minute. Heck, he felt like a real jerk whenever he told Kayla he didn't have time to read or just plain didn't want to. It wasn't like he was illiterate. He read just fine—quietly and to himself. But he still remembered the humiliation of stuttering over simple words when forced to perform in front of an audience: the snickers of kids who could read better than him, the way Mrs. Bridger cleared her throat and told him to start all over at the beginning of the passage.

His refusal to speak out loud in class served his pride well, but it also resulted in regular visits to the principal and hours of detention.

"Guess what," Kayla said to Maggie. "I already know my letters and sounds. And I'm not even in kindergarten yet."

His niece was smart; that was for darn sure. Rosa had tried to talk Jake into letting her start kindergarten this year, but he'd said no.

He'd told Rosa that Kayla needed time to get used to

the other changes in her life, which was true. But he worried about sending her off to school, especially with her disability, and wanted to protect her for as long as he could. Next year, when she was six, would be soon enough.

"After I get your brother cleaned up and the kitchen scrubbed down," Maggie said, "we can take time for a story or two."

Kayla clapped her hands. "I'm glad you came to help us."

Maggie slid Jake another teasing smile, one that suggested she intended to prod him until he took Sam and Kayla on his lap and read them a story each night before bedtime.

Before he could come up with a retort or change the subject, a shrill voice called from the entry.

"Yoo-hoo!"

Victoria Winston. Jake blew out a heavy breath. *Not her. Not now.*

"Jake, are you in the kitchen?" Victoria called.

Maggie raised her brows, asking, it seemed, for some kind of explanation, if not an introduction. But she'd figure it out soon enough.

"Yeah, Vickie. I'm in here."

Maggie watched, as an attractive woman dressed in designer Western wear sauntered into the kitchen, filling the room with a heavy dose of Chanel No. 5. Expensive denim hugged her hips, and a low-cut blouse flaunted perky breasts no bra could contain.

The tall, leggy brunette must be one of the wealthy guests of the ranch, Maggie suspected. But the sexually charged smile she slipped Jake indicated she was more than a guest.

Maggie crossed her arms. The faded jeans and old

sweatshirt she wore suddenly seemed blousy and over-sized, and she wished she would have taken time to at least put on some lipstick.

The woman scrunched a makeup laden face at the mess, but when she spotted Maggie, her smile lit up like a Macy's department store on Christmas Eve. "Oh! Looks like the baby-sitter finally arrived."

The baby-sitter? Had Jake told the woman that Maggie was coming to look after the children? Had he implied she was hired help and not just a friend offering a favor?

Vickie scanned the length of Maggie, smiling as though she'd passed some kind of inspection. She winked at Jake, in a sly, foxy way. "You should have a lot more free time now."

Maggie had a sudden urge to clobber them both, and she wasn't entirely sure why.

"Vickie, this is Dr. Templeton. She's a pediatrician and an old friend." Jake turned to Maggie. "This is one of our guests, Victoria Winston."

Vickie didn't seem to be the outdoor, dude ranch type. A high-class spa would seem to be her style. But her obvious attraction to Jake indicated she'd planned her vacation well.

It seemed this sly, female fox had a plan to capture a prize hound dog. It was an age-old game, and Maggie wondered whether Jake would take the bait.

Years ago, back when Maggie used to be a guest herself, one of the lady guests had made an obvious play for Jake's uncle. Maggie had always figured the lonely woman had set her sights on sleeping with a real live cowboy and signed up for a stint at the dude ranch with that sole purpose in mind.

Back then, she'd thought it kind of funny. But there didn't seem to be anything humorous about Vickie the vixen and her obvious attraction to the cowboy with his share of female conquests.

"Well, now," Vickie said. "A nanny with a medical degree is just the kind of sitter I'd hire, if I were inclined to have a few rugrats of my own."

Maggie doubted the woman would risk marring her body with stretch marks, let alone any of the other subtle differences brought on by childbirth. She seemed too showy, too self-absorbed, too groomed to perfection.

Vickie extended her arm, gold bangles clanging upon a sparkling tennis bracelet. "How do you do?"

Maggie took the proffered hand, noting the cool, silky texture and polished nails that boasted of regular manicures. "I'm fine, thank you."

"Jake, honey," Vickie said, batting mascara-thickened lashes. "Now you can take me on one of those late-night rides that was advertised in the brochure. Last time I asked, you mentioned not having someone to look after the kids." Tinted lips curled into a sly, take-me-to-bed smile.

The vixen turned to Maggie. "You work full-time, right? And the kiddies will be sleeping...."

Maggie shot a glance at Jake, wondering what he'd tell the busty, can't-wait-to-get-naked-in-the-moonlight brunette.

"Rosa's hospitalization has set me back. I've got a lot of things I need to do. I'm afraid the late-night ride is out of the question. Maybe next time."

A cherry-red bottom lip pooched out in a little-rich-girl pout.

What would Jake have told the vixen had Rosa not been out on disability? Had Maggie not been witness to the woman's blatant attempt to spend some late-night hours with the good-looking cowboy?

Sam squealed, then began to grunt and squirm out of the high chair.

"Would you mind watching the kids, Maggie?" Jake asked. "I need to talk to Vickie outside."

"By all means." Maggie feigned a smile as Jake and the vixen stepped out the back door.

Of all the… She'd meant to help Jake with the kids, make things easier on him, not so that he could find time to fraternize with the guests.

She grumbled while pulling out drawers until she found a dishcloth she could use to wash off at least some of the chocolate Sam wore like body paint, all the while mumbling under her breath.

At least she hadn't thought she'd spoken aloud.

"Did you say something about reindeer?" Kayla asked.

Maggie glanced over her shoulder at the girl. "Reindeer? No."

"But you said, 'Vixen,' and that's one of Santa's reindeer."

Maggie couldn't quell a wry grin from forming. "Yes, I suppose I did. That lady reminds me of a reindeer, the way she prances and dances around your uncle."

Kayla laughed. "Does Uncle Jake remind you of Santa Claus?"

"Not really," Maggie said. But she thought Victoria Winston was hoping to sit on Cowboy Claus's lap and get her name on his naughty-girl list. "Kayla, it was rude of me to think about that, let alone say it out loud. I'm sorry."

"That's okay," the little girl said. "I don't like her, either. She just walks in the house all the time, even when the other people are doing fun stuff like riding and swimming."

That didn't surprise Maggie. Victoria Winston had set her sights on good old Uncle Jake.

She wondered whether the hound dog would succumb to temptation.

Vickie sidled up to Jake as he escorted her outside and down the walk toward the barn.

He sidestepped her. "I've made it a point not to date or become involved with any of the guests at Buckaroo Ranch."

"Why's that?" she asked, closing the space he'd tried to put between them. "I'm not asking for any kind of commitment. Maybe just a visit or two to my cabin late at night, when the others are sound asleep. Don't tell me you haven't thought about it."

It was hard not to think about sex in front of Vickie. She all but wore a sign around her neck saying Ready, Willing and More Than Able. But shoot, he was a family man now. A role model, albeit a tarnished one.

"Oh," she said, noticing something on Jake's face and licking her finger. "What's this? Looks like chocolate. I'll get it off for you." She rubbed the skin above his brow, then slipped an index finger into her mouth, wrapping her tongue around it and slowly pulling it out. "Mmm. Good."

Her eyes told him she wanted to taste more than chocolate.

Was everything a sexual innuendo with the woman? Part of the fun of having sex was in the chase. Vickie didn't let a guy get out of the starting blocks.

She gave him a kiss upon the forehead, right where the chocolate had supposedly been. "Think about it, honey. You won't be sorry."

He was sorry already. High-maintenance women like

Vickie were a dime a dozen. He'd become adept at kindly brushing off their propositions, but he wasn't used to dealing with them in front of his niece and Maggie.

Vickie was pushing his patience to the limit.

"What about the party on Friday? Surely you can find time for a dance."

The hayride and barn dance were the highlight of a Buckaroo week. As long as Jake had committed to fulfilling the reservations his sister had made over a year ago, the weekly event would go on as planned.

"All right," he told her. "One dance."

But something told him that wouldn't be enough for Victoria Winston.

Now if he could just get the woman to go back to her cabin or encourage her to have a facial. Maybe catch one of the sunset rides into the canyon. But he doubted that any of his suggestions would work and opted to bow out gracefully. "You'll have to excuse me, Vickie. I've got to get things lined up inside. Then I have a lot of work to catch up on."

"Sure, Jake, I'll excuse you. But don't forget about the dance on Friday night."

"No, I won't forget." Jake tipped his hat, then headed back to the house.

When he stepped inside the kitchen, Maggie was busy wiping Sam's face and hands. She had her back to him and didn't speak when he entered. Something told him that wasn't a good thing.

Kayla, on the other hand, giggled out loud.

"What's so funny?" he asked.

"You got a big, red, reindeer kiss on your face."

Chapter Four

A reindeer kiss?

Jake didn't know where Kayla had come up with that, but he knew what she was talking about and quickly wiped where Vickie had left her mark.

Maggie, who had turned at Kayla's reindeer comment, wore a weird smile, one that poked a teasing accusation at his conscience.

But what did he have to feel guilty about? It wasn't his fault that Vickie was doing her best to stake an unwelcome claim on him. He couldn't think of anything to say in his defense, so he didn't utter a word and continued to wipe at the damn lipstick.

Maggie handed him a paper towel. "Don't let us keep you from joining in the reindeer games."

Kayla giggled, although he *still* wasn't sure where the reindeer came in, since Christmas was three months away. But Kayla had a vivid imagination and was always several steps ahead of him. Apparently, Maggie was sharp enough to keep up with her.

"If you're talking about the red-lipped reindeer," he said, "I'm not interested in her games."

Kayla and Maggie shot each other a conspiratorial glance, and Jake wondered whether he'd be able to keep up with either of them. "I've got chores to do. Are you two going to be okay?"

"Sure." Maggie tossed Kayla a gentle smile. "We'll be just fine without you."

Jake had no doubt about that.

He studied Maggie as she stood near the high chair. She wore a yellow sweatshirt with a college logo and a pair of faded jeans. Caramel eyes that could lure a man to their depths glimmered, and hair the color of golden corn silk brushed her shoulders. She smiled in a playful way that made a guy want to step closer, to fill the gap between them. Full, unpainted lips begged to be kissed and promised not to leave lipstick smears all over a man's face. Or anywhere else they might choose to touch.

His mind drifted to the kiss they'd shared in Boston. It hadn't been much, as far as kisses went, just a sensual hint that blazed with passion. It had been a ploy, an act meant to imply he and Maggie were lovers. Jake had figured the kiss would surprise the sophisticated, scholarly types who had attended the hospital benefit. But it had surprised him more than anyone.

He hadn't expected it to turn him every which way but loose, but it had. And he'd laughed it off, rather than allow himself to take it further, to see how Maggie would respond to a real kiss, one meant to entice her.

One meant to entice them both.

Jake shook off the urge to kiss her again, to take their attraction to a deeper level. Dr. Maggie Templeton, he reminded himself, was definitely off-limits, no matter how wholesome and kissable she looked. "If you'll excuse me, I've got work to do."

"Sure," Maggie said.

He had the strangest urge to grab her in his arms and kiss her, just to let her know that he found her far more attractive than the sex-starved ranch guest.

Instead, Jake left the house before he did something really stupid.

A full moon hovered over the darkened Texas countryside, as Maggie stood on the porch and leaned against the polished oak railing.

Kayla and Sam had finally drifted off to sleep, their tummies full of chicken noodle soup, sliced apples and grilled cheese sandwiches.

A light from the dining room, an outbuilding that also held a state-of-the-art kitchen, burned bright, indicating the guests were still in the throes of after-dinner conversation. She supposed she could have joined them for the evening meal, like Jake had suggested when he came in to check on the kids, but it was his place to be with the guests. And besides, she preferred to eat with the children.

A lone figure in boots and hat stepped out of the dining room and sauntered toward the house.

Jake.

"Hey, Magpie," he said with a slow, steady drawl. "Are Sam and Kayla asleep?"

"Finally." She managed a weary smile. "You're a lucky man, Jake. They're really neat kids."

"Yeah, they're super." He climbed the porch and stood by her side, close enough to touch, close enough to cloak her in his musky scent. "Did they give you any trouble?"

"No, not really. Sam is an energetic little guy, but he

wound down about an hour ago. I found him asleep on the floor by the toy box.''

"He climbs out of his crib. Rosa doesn't make much of a fuss about his bedtime, because he usually nods off early, but not in his own bed. I just pick him up where I find him and carry him to his room.''

They stood quiet for a moment, lost in their own thoughts, Maggie presumed, although hers weren't centered on anything specific, just the twinkling stars, the occasional whinny of a horse in pasture and the masculine aura of the cowboy beside her.

"Shame, isn't it?" he said.

"What is?"

"That someone would take this beautiful land and turn it into a dude ranch for rich city slickers.''

"Those city slickers pay good money to vacation here.''

"I know. But sometimes, they drive me nuts. Like today.''

She supposed he was talking about Vickie. "It must be flattering to have the ladies flock around you.''

He turned slowly, snagging her gaze in his. "Women like Vickie don't impress me. They're more trouble than they're worth.''

"What kind of women impress you?" she asked, unable to keep the question to herself.

He ran his knuckles along her cheek, sending a heated shiver to her bones. "Women like you, Maggie. But I make it a point to steer clear of them, too.''

Something grazed her heart, made her want to believe he actually found her attractive and wasn't just being a nice guy, an appreciative friend.

She smiled. "And why is that? Are women like me more trouble than we're worth?''

"Not you, Magpie." He brushed her cheek with a whispery kiss, one that made her want to reach for the lapel of the light, denim jacket he wore and pull him face-to-face. Mouth-to-mouth.

She crossed her arms, and he turned to scan the grounds, leaving her alone with her fantasy.

"You know what I'd like to do with this place?" His voice held a wistful note, and she realized it was the first time he'd ever indicated he had a dream, a goal of some kind.

"What's that?"

"I'd like to turn it into a real ranch. Run some cattle. Train horses bred for more than trail riding."

"Why don't you?"

He shrugged. "Maybe I will, after I honor all the paid reservations my sister had already accepted."

They stood silent again, listening to crickets chirp in the crisp night air.

Maggie couldn't help but close her eyes and relish the faint scent of a woodsy aftershave that mingled with leather and musk. She really couldn't blame the vixen for wanting to sleep with Jake; what woman wouldn't?

A warm glow surrounded the dining-room windows, while a smoky swirl rose from the stone fireplace and disappeared into the night sky.

"Looks like the guests are still going strong," Maggie said. "You didn't leave early because of me, did you?"

"No. I left because Vickie wouldn't leave me alone, and I'm not into public displays of affection."

She thought of the display Jake had put on for her colleagues in Boston and realized he'd performed the public act as a favor to her. It made her appreciate his efforts all the more. And made her more resentful of the vixen's blatant seduction attempts. "I think Vickie's looking for a private showing of affection."

"Yeah, but even though I'm not into forever-type commitments, I keep my relationships private. Vickie isn't very discreet." He lifted his hat and raked a hand through his hair. "Believe it or not, I'm not interested."

"Good," Maggie said. "She may be wealthy, but she's just plain tacky. Kayla and I don't think she's your type."

He chuckled. "You and Kayla seem to have hit it off pretty well."

"We have. She's a wonderful little girl—bright and entertaining. And it seems that her handicap has only strengthened her spirit."

"And her will. She's a tough little cookie."

"I suppose so, but she's a loving cookie. And a devoted sister to Sam."

He cleared his throat, and she had a feeling he was going to change the subject. "I'm going to try and get a sitter for Friday night. Sara, Rosa's daughter, will be home from college. If she's available, I'll ask her."

"Why's that? I can watch the kids."

Jake slipped an arm around her shoulders and gave her a quick, brotherly hug. "I don't want you to miss the hayride and dance."

"I came to help," Maggie said, wishing he hadn't removed his arm so soon.

"I know, but it feels weird knowing you're going to be changing diapers and chasing after kids all day long. I want you to have a break."

"I don't expect to take part in the guest activities." A cool breeze kicked up, and Maggie inadvertently rubbed the goose bumps on her arms.

"You're cold." He slipped his arm around her again, this time pulling her close.

It seemed so natural to lean into him, to share body heat. She tilted her head to the side, resting it upon his shoulder. With Jake beside her, the night sounds seemed louder and more pronounced, the scents more fragrant, the evening more enjoyable.

"It's a beautiful ranch," Maggie said. "I don't think I ever appreciated it before."

"I guess I still don't. As far as I'm concerned, it's a waste of good land and stock." Jake blew out a sigh. "Once I left home, I avoided this place as often as I could. Who would have guessed that the whole damn thing would be dumped in my lap?"

"You said you'd like to make it into a working ranch," Maggie reminded him.

"Yeah. Someday."

When Maggie opened her mouth to respond, a yawn forced its way out.

"Tired?" he asked.

"It's been a long day."

"Come on." Jake dropped his arm and took her by the hand. "Let's go to bed."

It sounded like such a married thing to say. Such a natural thing to do.

Let's go to bed.

She actually found herself wondering what it would be like, had Jake meant that they should go to bed together.

Maggie wasn't in the mood for a hayride or a barn dance, but Jake had insisted.

He thought she needed a break from the kids, but she actually enjoyed taking care of them. Sam, of course, kept her running, but he was a happy little boy, full of love and affection. And Kayla was both precocious and entertaining.

"You're off duty," he told her when the sitter arrived.

She'd intended to argue, to insist upon staying at home with the children, but Sam had squealed in delight when Rosa's daughter walked through the door. And Kayla had hurried to reach the pretty college student, an assortment of questions about Rosa spilling from her mouth.

Consequently, Maggie found herself seated on a bale of straw, next to a husband and wife from a Los Angeles suburb. Along with the other guests, they watched the setting sun paint the sky in streaks of orange, purple and blue. A flock of crows chattered to each other in the cottonwood trees, while two colts frolicked in the pasture nearby.

"You'll like California," Bev Cummings said. "The weather is to die for. And so is the beach."

"Cost of real estate is high," her husband, Ben added. "But not a bad investment, by any means. The price isn't going anywhere but up, especially if you live near the coast."

"I can't wait to move," Maggie said, although her attention wasn't focused on the friendly Southern California natives.

Instead, she watched Vickie snuggle up to Jake, flirting and making her intentions more than obvious to the others on the hay wagon. The woman wore skintight jeans, more jewelry than was called for and a low-cut blouse that revealed saline-enhanced breasts. Several of the men found her witty and entertaining.

Maggie didn't.

She glanced down at her boots, a pair of Sharon's that Jake had insisted she wear. Why had she agreed to come along? She'd never enjoyed this sort of thing.

"Jake, honey," Vickie said. "What does a cowboy like you do for fun?"

Maggie really didn't know what Jake Honey did for fun, but she had this incredible urge to boot Vickie off the wagon—just for fun.

"I don't have much free time anymore," Jake said.

"That's too bad. You know what they say about all work and no play...." The vixen patted the inside of Jake's thigh.

Maggie'd had her fill of hayrides and red-lipped reindeer. And as for the barn dance? No, thank you. She'd come up with a credible excuse. There was no way she'd sit and watch Vickie make a fool of herself by panting all over a cowboy who was too damn sexy for his own good.

As the wagon pulled up to the barn, country music sounded from within.

Jake slid off the straw bale, his feet hitting the ground before anyone else could climb down.

Vickie reached out her arms. "Help me, would you, honey?"

Maggie would have been more than happy to help Vickie, with a well-placed kick to her denim-coated buttocks.

With more grace than Maggie expected, Jake helped Vickie down, while disentangling himself from her clutches.

Maggie climbed from the wagon without assistance, then turned to head back to the house. Vickie's game had become much too tiring to watch. She'd rather chat with Sara and the kids in the house.

"Hey," Jake called out. "Where do you think you're going?"

She stopped, then slowly turned. "I think I'll pass on the rest of the evening's festivities."

"Don't you dare leave me alone with her."

"Maybe you should just tell that oversexed woman

with the tenacity of a bulldog that she's barking up the wrong tree.''

''I have. In so many words.'' Jake sighed, and Maggie actually felt sorry for him. ''I guess she's not used to a man telling her he's not interested.''

''When does she check out?''

''Sunday morning, thank goodness.''

''Well, surely you can handle another day and a half.'' Maggie started to turn, and Jake grabbed her hand.

''Let's resume our act.''

''Our act?''

''You know,'' he said with a crooked smile. ''The one where we pretend to be lovers.''

Maggie's heart tumbled around in her chest like a tennis shoe in the dryer. ''You want to pretend there's something between us? Again?''

''It worked for you in Boston.''

It had, Maggie realized. But how much more pretending could her senses handle?

He took her hand and gave it a gentle squeeze. ''Come on inside, Magpie. We'll give Vickie a show and let her know she doesn't stand a chance of turning my head.''

Maggie blew out a soft sigh while she tried to come up with a good reason for declining his request, but couldn't think of one she wanted to share with Jake. She certainly didn't want to tell him she was struggling with an unwelcome attraction to him.

''All right,'' she said with reluctance.

''Thanks, Magpie.'' Jake drew her into the barn, where lanterns lit the room in a nostalgic, down-home glow and feet tapped to the sounds of a lively fiddle.

Vickie, surrounded by two male guests trying to vie for her attention, perked up when Jake and Maggie entered. If Jake thought that having Maggie on his arm would slow down the vixen's interest, he had another think coming. She flashed him a pearly white smile and waved from across the room. Her gold bangles jingle-jangled like a gypsy tambourine.

"I don't think the 'act' will work with that woman," Maggie said.

Jake slowed his steps, then spun Maggie around to face him. "You've got the wrong attitude, Magpie. And you're wearing the wrong expression."

"What do you mean by that?"

He cupped her face, his thumbs making slow, sensual strokes on her cheeks. Their eyes caught, and her heart did a swan dive into her tummy. How could that man rustle up heat and desire like that? Gee whiz, if Maggie didn't know this was just an act, she'd think he was ready to carry her to bed.

"That's better." His lip curled on one side in that cocky, bad-boy style.

How could her expression be better than before? "I'm not smiling."

"No. But you've got that sex-glazed look in your eyes." He lifted her chin with the calloused tip of a finger. "Lick your lips."

As though mesmerized, she did as he asked. For goodness' sake, she felt like an untried virgin in the hands of a cowboy Adonis. What was he planning to do? She hadn't a clue, but she let him take the lead.

He lowered his mouth to hers, and for some silly reason—maybe just plain anticipation—she whimpered before their lips touched. Had she not been so caught up in the moment, her reaction might have embarrassed her.

She expected the kiss to be just like the one they'd shared at the hospital benefit in Boston—one light in touch, but laced heavily with sexual intent.

And that's how the kiss started.

He brushed his lips against hers, once, twice. But when her mouth parted in reaction to being so sensuously touched, he deepened the intimacy, teasing her tongue with his. Lordy, how that man could kiss.

The bones in her legs turned to cartilage, so it seemed, and she feared she'd fall to the straw-littered floor if she didn't hang on for dear life. And hang on, she did.

Her thoughts spun out of control, and heat pooled low in her belly, jump-starting her libido into overdrive. Had Jake not ended the kiss, she feared she would have continued until one or the other begged for fulfillment.

"Hot damn, Magpie. You sure know how to kiss a man like you mean it."

She knew how to kiss? Not really, but Jake Meredith was darn sure teaching her how it was done.

"Come on, let's dance."

Dance? She didn't want to dance. She wanted to take him around to the back of the barn and make out under the stars like a couple of moonstruck teenagers. Shoot, she wanted to do more than make out. And if she were seventeen again, and innocent, she would have gladly given him her virginity and anything else he might want to take.

As the band began to play a country love song, Jake drew Maggie out onto the dance floor and took her into his arms. The scents of her perfume blended with his woodsy cologne, as they swayed to the sensual beat. Had the music not ended, and Jake not let go, Maggie might have held him forever.

Jake took her hand and led her from the dance floor. He leaned his head close to hers. "You're one hell of an actress, Magpie. Everyone in this room will think we've got something going."

Will they? Maggie feigned a smile. If truth be told, she feared her acting skills had very little to do with anything.

The desire she felt for Jake Meredith was becoming a little too realistic and stimulating for her own good.

Chapter Five

Jake adjusted his Stetson as he led Maggie from the dance floor. He'd tried to make light of the last kiss they'd shared, but the fact was, it had been nearly too hot for comfort.

Too hot? He was still smoldering.

He'd had to dance with Maggie, just to keep his arousal hidden until it subsided. But since she kept leaning into him, taunting a demanding erection, he wasn't sure whether he'd been able to conceal it from her.

Did she realize how badly he'd wanted to make love to her? How badly he still wanted to?

Jake grumbled under his breath. Maggie had a way of burrowing into his heart and soul. At least, she always had. For that reason alone, keeping her at arm's distance would be tough enough. But sex had a way of making a woman want more of a guy than he was willing to share.

After making small talk with the guests, Jake and Maggie headed back to the house. They entered the living room where Sara and the children had gathered by the fireplace. Sara held an open storybook, and even Sam had given her his undivided attention.

Great. Sam was going to be another avid reader who would soon start bugging Jake to read out loud.

"Oh, goody, Uncle Jake." Kayla said. "You're back. I was afraid you wouldn't come home until I was sound asleep, and then I couldn't ask you."

"Ask me what?"

Kayla climbed down from Sara's lap, and awkwardly made her way toward him. It tore at his heart to see her stilted gait, yet her determination amazed him and made him proud.

"Rosa isn't at the hospital anymore. And Sara said we could go visit her, if it's okay with you. So will it be okay?" Kayla looked at him with cocker spaniel eyes. "Please?"

He'd been afraid she was going to ask for something unreasonable. "Of course you can visit Rosa. She's probably missed you as much as you two have missed her."

"She sure has," Sara said, setting Sam onto the floor and handing him the book. "Mom can't wait to come back to work."

Jake couldn't wait for Rosa to come back to work, either. Not just to help with the kids, but things were backing up in the office, and he depended upon her to help him keep on top of things.

"I'll pick them up tomorrow morning," Sara said. "Is eleven o'clock all right?"

"Sure." Jake watched Sara kiss the kids then reach for her backpack.

She paused in the doorway. "Jake, anytime I'm in town, I'll be glad to watch Sam and Kayla."

"That's good to know." He pulled a twenty from his wallet and handed it to the college student. "Thanks for coming out here tonight."

"No problem." Sara said goodbye to Maggie and the kids, then left the house.

"All right," Maggie said to Sam and Kayla. "It's late. Let's go to bed."

Bedtime.

The kids would get a kiss good-night, a hug and a prayer.

But what would Jake get? He'd already had the kiss and hug.

And as for prayers?

He certainly could use a few of those, because he was going to need divine help in order to survive sleeping just two doors down the hall from Maggie, especially if he didn't want to crumble under the powerful urge to take her to bed.

His bed.

Could he hold out for six to eight weeks?

Not without a ton of cold showers.

Maggie glanced at the clock on the fireplace mantel— 2:00 a.m. Hours before dawn.

Outside the warmth of the den, the autumn wind rustled the trees, and a steady rain tapped upon the windowpanes. She wished she could say the weather had kept her awake, but that wasn't true. If her mind hadn't been so disturbed by thoughts of a certain cowboy, she would have dozed off hours ago.

She sat on the leather sofa, legs tucked under her and an afghan lying across her lap. The novel she'd found on the bookshelf must have belonged to Sharon. Maggie would have preferred a murder mystery to a historical romance, particularly because she needed to direct her thoughts away from ruggedly handsome rogues and their fair ladies, but that's all she'd been able to find.

Footsteps sounded in the hall, and she looked up to see Jake standing in the doorway in his bare feet. He wore only a pair of gray sweatpants—no shirt, just broad shoulders and a golden suntan. A muscular chest sported a thatch of dark hair that narrowed over washboard abs and became a line that disappeared into the waistband of his sweats.

When she lifted her gaze from where it shouldn't have strayed, his sterling blue eyes caught hers. She swallowed hard, hoping he hadn't detected her mouthwatering reaction at seeing him so sleep-tousled. Get a grip, she told herself while trying to give him an unaffected smile that wouldn't betray her sexually charged thoughts.

He slid her a crooked grin, and her cheeks warmed.

"What are you doing up?" she asked, trying to hide her reaction to the sight of him. Had thoughts of her kept him awake, too? A childish, dreamy part of her wished they had.

"I couldn't sleep. Looks like you couldn't, either."

Maggie wasn't about to tell Jake that thoughts of that last kiss had kept her awake for hours. "The rain woke me."

He nodded. "Me, too. I was going to get something to drink. Can I bring you something? Hot chocolate maybe?"

"Sure. That sounds good."

Jake flashed her a dazzling smile. For a moment, she wanted to drag him back to the sofa and make out like a teenage couple who finally had the house to themselves.

Oh, for goodness' sake. How could he stir up those adolescent urges? Maggie scanned the open novel, trying to find the place where she'd left off reading, but for the life of her couldn't get back into the story. When Jake returned to the study with two steaming cups of hot cocoa, Maggie made room for him to join her on the sofa.

"Thanks again for coming to help me out," Jake said.

Was he talking about her helping him with the kids or with keeping the vixen at bay? Maybe both. "You're welcome."

"I want to do right by the kids, but the whole domestic scene has me unbalanced. I'm not a family man. Never have been."

Maggie assumed his past had something to do with it. But he was a family man now, whether he liked it or not. "I admire you for trying to do what's best for Sam and Kayla. You might not feel capable of parenting them, but you are."

Jake took a slow sip of the chocolate. "If my dad had been a better role model, maybe I'd feel better."

Things at home had gotten bad just before his dad died and Jake had moved to Buckaroo Ranch to live with his uncle, but Maggie remembered him telling her about his life in the earlier years, before his mother's death. His life hadn't always been tough. "You'll have to rely on the good memories to see you through."

Jake grew solemn, more pensive than usual. "At first, before my mom died, he was a pretty good dad, I guess. He taught me how to ride and rope. We had a good time together—at least whenever he wasn't on the rodeo circuit. But after Mom passed on, and he was strapped with taking care of Sharon and I, things changed. That's when he started drinking."

Maggie knew Jake's dad had been an alcoholic, just as her stepdad had been. It was one of the things they'd had in common that very first summer they'd met. It was also one of the things they'd dealt with—in different ways. Jake had experimented with drinking, while Maggie had campaigned against it.

One summer day, while they'd fished in the old swimming hole, Jake had pulled out a bottle of Jack Daniel's and poured it into his cola can.

"I'd think you would avoid whiskey, especially since your dad had such a problem with it," Maggie had said.

Jake had tossed her a half shrug, then took a swig. "Must be something magical about this stuff, don't you think?"

Maggie hadn't found anything magical about alcohol, at least not in the fairy-tale sense. Her stepfather put away a case of beer every night, and the only magic she saw was the Jekyll and Hyde transformation that made a halfway decent man turn into an ogre.

She looked at the man sitting next to her, remembering the sullen boy he once had been. "I used to worry about your drinking. I was afraid you'd follow in your father's staggering footsteps."

"Yeah," he said. "You used to harp at me about it. I guess it sank in, Magpie."

She smiled. "I'm glad."

Jake was glad, too. He'd told Maggie before that his old man had drank himself to death. In a sense, he had. But Jake still felt a powerful sense of guilt over it all, which was one of the reasons he hadn't ever wanted a family of his own—the reason why he feared he'd let down anyone who depended upon him.

Maggie had suggested he focus on the good memories, but how could he when it was the more recent ones that haunted him, that still poked a calloused finger at his chest and glared at him with bloodshot eyes?

And if the memories of his dad didn't taunt him into

believing he'd failed, Uncle Dave's accusations did. *You're a damn troublemaker, Jake. Why can't you be a good kid, like your sister? No wonder the school has damn near given up on you. You'll never amount to a hill of beans.*

The past had a lousy way of sneaking up on a guy, of throwing stuff in his face and making him hurt all over again.

Was that what it had been like for his dad? Were those the kind of memories his father had drank to forget?

Or had his dad just resented being stuck with a kid like Jake?

He tossed Maggie a weak smile. "My dad never could handle his problems. That's why he tried to drown them with ninety proof."

"That kind of fix is only temporary," she said, "and the problems come back tenfold."

Jake's thoughts drifted to the night his father died. The night the booze hadn't been enough. And the night Jake had really let his old man down.

"Come here, boy," his dad had said, words slurring. "I wanna talk to you." Bobby Joe Meredith had always wanted to talk when he was liquored up. And he'd repeat himself, oftentimes making no sense whatsoever.

"I don't want to talk, Dad. I'm tired." Jake had rolled over in bed and put the pillow over his head. Why was he the one his old man wanted to talk to? His dad never woke Sharon to talk, which was probably why she never got sent to the principal's office for sleeping in class.

"I'm hurtin', son."

Jake had ignored his words. He'd heard them all before. And he'd seen the tears, too. Bobby Joe Meredith wasn't just drunk and talkative that night, he was on a crying binge, too. Jake had sat through too many of those senseless ramblings in the past and wasn't up for another all-night marathon. "Pour yourself another drink, Dad."

And that's what Bobby Joe had done. But instead of blacking out until morning, he'd taken a permanent escape.

"You're right," Jake told Maggie. "The problems don't ever go away. And sometimes they dog a man's son for the rest of his life."

"What do you mean?" she asked.

Jake didn't know why he'd opened that can of worms. He really didn't want to discuss it. It was one of the things he'd kept buried inside, but for some reason he wanted to share some of it with Maggie. "I told you my old man drank himself to death. But to be perfectly honest, he got drunk one night and killed himself."

Maggie slid closer and took his hand in hers. She didn't say anything, just let him know she was there for him, like she'd always done in the past. But what would she do if she knew the guilt he harbored? If she knew that Jake had failed his father. That Jake wasn't the kind of son a man could depend on; he wasn't the kind of guy anyone should depend on.

"I didn't do a damn thing to help him." He waited for her to respond, knowing she'd try to take the guilt away, try to make him feel better about things. But it wouldn't work.

Her thumb caressed the top of his hand. "Surviving family members and friends often blame themselves following a suicide. Your dad needed to reach out for help."

"He reached out," Jake said. "And I refused to listen to him."

"How old were you?"

"Twelve and a half."

Maggie squeezed his hand. "Come on, Jake. You were a kid. It wasn't your fault."

"You're right," he told her, even though he still wasn't convinced. He should have sat up all night, like he had in the past, listening until the old man drank himself into a stupor and the suicidal urge had passed. Maggie might have a point, but Jake would continue to blame himself. It's all he knew how to do.

"If you need to talk about it—"

"I don't." He didn't know why he'd mentioned it now and wished he hadn't. As always, whenever anyone got too close to the junk he kept locked away, a change of subject was in order.

Jake stood, wandered to the window and peered out into the rainy night. "Can you imagine this place without any city slickers?"

"Yes. And I'm glad you can, too."

He turned and caught her smile, but didn't speak.

"This is the first time you've ever had a goal. Well," she corrected, "it's the first time you've mentioned one to me."

Yeah, well, he'd had plenty of goals in the past, just not any that were possible for a guy like him to achieve, other than being a damn good rodeo cowboy. But Sharon's death had curtailed that. No way would he have dragged those two kids around while he rode the circuit. He knew firsthand how tough that kind of life was. Living out of duffel bags, moving from place to place. Never settling down long enough to make friends. It hadn't seemed to bother his sister, though. She'd just stuck her nose in a book and poured her energy into making good grades and pleasing every teacher who came in and out of her life.

Sometimes Jake wondered if he'd ever stayed at one

school long enough, whether some teacher might have figured out a way to reach a kid like him. If so, he might have stuck it out. But then again, maybe he was just too ornery to stay focused, like old Mrs. Bridger had said.

"Sam and Kayla are lucky to have you." Maggie, her eyes full of admiration and other mushy stuff he didn't deserve, smiled. "You're talented with horses and should utilize the gifts you were blessed with. I'm sure you'll turn Buckaroo Ranch into something to be proud of."

He appreciated her encouragement and didn't have the heart to spill all of his misgivings. "Well, we'll just have to see how things pan out."

"So," Maggie said. "Is that why you can't sleep? Too caught up in plans for the future?"

She looked hopeful, and he didn't have the guts to admit he was plagued by worries of the future—not hopes and dreams. And he damn sure wasn't going to confess to having insomnia because memories of the hot kisses they'd shared continued to stimulate him. "Yep. That's why I can't sleep."

"Let me give you a neck and shoulder rub. Come here."

Against his better judgment, Jake complied, taking a seat on the sofa and letting Maggie's fingers work their magic on his skin. She massaged his neck and shoulders, kneading the tenseness from his muscles, but not relaxing him into a weary state. Not by any means. The heat of her touch sharpened his senses, waking him with needs he wasn't about to sate with Maggie.

The scent of her shampoo, something floral and fresh, made him want to bury his nose in her hair, then kiss his way down her neck. As she worked to free the knots in his shoulders, her breaths came in soft, whispery puffs, making him want to turn and take her mouth with his, taste those little pants and match them with his own.

She leaned forward, and the fullness of her breasts pressed against his shoulder blade. A pebbled nipple indicated Maggie had found the massage as stimulating as he did. How much more of this could he take without facing her and acknowledging the state of his arousal?

Not much more. He turned and recognized desire in her eyes. He might not have done anything, other than move away and put some distance between them, if she hadn't parted her lips.

They were both going to be sorry for this, but there wasn't a damn thing he could do about it now. He wanted to kiss her too badly, wanted to stake some kind of claim, even if it wouldn't last.

When their lips met, her mouth opened, allowing the kiss to deepen into the kind they'd both been hungry to taste. Tongues mated, and she reached her hands into his hair and guided his face closer, his tongue deeper into her mouth.

Had any other woman tasted as sweet? Tempted him beyond reason? No. And he doubted another ever would.

He wanted to press himself against her, let her know how much he wanted her. The attraction he'd tried so hard to ignore ignited into a full-blown passion and threatened to burn out of control. He wanted to lay her down and bury himself deep within her, but as badly as Jake wanted to make love to Maggie, he couldn't let things get to the point of no return. He had to stop.

It took all he had to break the kiss, and when he pulled away, he feared he wouldn't be able to help himself from taking her back into his arms again.

But how could he do that when Maggie was worming her way into his soul? He'd never let a woman get that kind of a hold on him before. And he sure as hell couldn't risk it with Maggie. "I…uh…guess we took things a bit too far."

Too far? Maggie wondered.

Or not far enough.

With her heart racing and mind reeling, Maggie tried to gain some composure. What in the world had she been thinking? She knew better than to let a kiss get out of control like that. Especially with a man who could win an Academy Award for Best Actor, a man who changed lovers as casually as he changed expressions.

"I don't know what got into me," she said. Although she feared she did. Jake had teased her senses until lust took over, completely upending any sign of reason.

An affair might threaten the friendship they'd built. And even if she could believe Jake was capable of feeling something special for her, that he might be able to commit to something long-term and lasting, she'd worked too hard to earn a medical degree.

What kind of future did Buckaroo Ranch hold for her? The nearest hospital was nearly an hour away. To even think of a permanent relationship with Jake was ridiculous. She'd have to give up all she'd worked for. All she had become.

He raked a hand through his hair. "I'm sorry, Magpie. You're just coming off a nasty divorce. And you're vulnerable right now. I won't take advantage of you by acting on this crazy attraction we feel."

He was right. She was vulnerable and wounded. That's why she hadn't been strong enough to stop things before they got out of hand. She was a woman with physical needs that hadn't been fulfilled in a long time.

And Jake was a good-looking cowboy who probably

knew how to draw a star-bursting climax out of a woman without even touching her.

"Thanks," she said. "Making love would take our friendship to a place neither of us needs to be."

He nodded in agreement. "That's right, honey."

"Well," she said, standing and trying to distance herself from the half-naked cowboy on the sofa. "I suppose I'd better go to bed. Sam and Kayla will be raring to go in a few short hours. I need to get some sleep."

"Me, too," he said, although he didn't stand or make a move indicating he was going anywhere.

"Good night, Jake." Maggie turned and walked away.

Sexual frustration and regret followed her out the doorway and back into her bedroom.

It would be another long, restless night.

Chapter Six

The rain stopped during midmorning, leaving a rainbow arched across patches of blue on a silver-clouded sky.

"Oh, goody," Kayla said, peering out the dining room window and fogging the glass. "We can go outside and play."

"I'm afraid not," Maggie told her. "It's too wet and muddy."

Kayla continued to beg, but Maggie remained steadfast in her decision. Finally the child turned away from where she'd been gazing at the swing and slide awaiting her in the backyard and trudged into the living room like a forlorn waif.

Several times during the morning Kayla pleaded her case, insisting the grounds were dry enough to play, and each time Maggie tried to direct her attention to indoor activities.

After lunch and Sam's nap, Kayla found Maggie in the

kitchen and again asked to go outside. "The sun's been shining, and I'll bet the mud is all dried up. I promise not to get dirty."

Maggie glanced out the window, noting the puddles of water in the backyard. "I'm sorry, honey. Maybe tomorrow."

Kayla sighed, her lips forming a perfect pout, just as Jake scraped his boots at the service porch and opened the kitchen door. He placed his hat upon the rack attached to the kitchen wall.

His hair, mussed and dampened by perspiration, seemed to magnify his rebellious image. A smudge of dried mud on his angular chin taunted Maggie to step close and brush it away—a reaction she deemed too intimate. Instead, she merely crossed her arms while her gaze remained transfixed upon the cowboy.

"The rain and wind weren't that hard last night, but an old oak tree in the south pasture fell on the fence. I've got it jerry-rigged for now, but I need a couple of new posts." He strode for the sink and turned on the water.

While he washed the evidence of his labor from his hands, Maggie studied his back. He wore a faded chambray shirt, a pair of washed-out jeans and scuffed boots. He looked every bit like the rugged cowboy he was. For some reason she'd rather not acknowledge, she found him far more handsome and appealing than any of the well-dressed doctors and professionals she'd known in Boston.

Jake snatched a paper towel from the spool, looked first at Maggie, then his niece. "Have you ladies had a nice day?"

"No," Kayla said. "It's been awful."

Quickly pushing aside her unwelcome attraction to Jake, Maggie grabbed hold of reality. Adult reinforcement had arrived.

Or so she hoped. Jake wouldn't agree to let the kids play in the mud, would he? She crossed her arms and allowed the conversation to play out.

"What's the matter?" Jake asked the child. "Did Sam get into your doll collection again?"

"No." Kayla clicked her tongue. "There's nothing to do. And Maggie won't let us go out and play."

"I don't blame her. It's too wet." Jake dried his hands, then tossed the used paper towel into the trash.

"But I already watched television and read hundreds of books and colored a zillion pictures." Kayla crossed her arms. "The only thing left to do is go outside."

Maggie had actually considered giving in, just to keep Kayla quiet, but as a pediatrician, she'd counseled many parents on standing firm. She just hadn't realized how tough that was to do in reality.

Packed in one of the storage crates, Maggie had a great book that suggested ways to keep housebound children busy. Even though she'd recommended it to parents on a regular basis, she'd never read the thing cover to cover— a big mistake.

"I've got to drive into town and make a stop at the lumberyard and the feed store," Jake said to Maggie. "That probably doesn't sound too exciting, but if you guys need some different scenery, you can come along."

Kayla clapped her hands. "I love to go to the feed store. They have chickens and ducks. It's almost like going to the zoo. Please, Maggie. Please say yes."

Jake laughed and placed a hand on Maggie's shoulder, a warm gesture that drew her into a familylike circle. "It's up to you."

Frankly, a trip to the mall, the art museum or the theatre was more to her liking, but anything sounded better than sitting inside the house with a bored child. Maggie grinned. "Sure. Why not?"

Five minutes later, Sam and Kayla sat securely in the back seat of Jake's dual-wheeled Chevy pickup, while Maggie climbed in front and buckled the seatbelt.

"Bye-bye!" Sam said, obviously happy to be included in the family outing.

The family outing.

Maggie should feel like an interloper. Instead, she felt a warm but surreal sense of belonging.

If only for today.

As they drove away from the ranch, Maggie settled back in her seat and enjoyed the ride.

Jake stopped by the lumberyard first, just to get the most boring part of the trip out of the way. Fortunately, no one complained while he purchased the new fence posts and placed them in the back of the truck. Moments later, they were headed to the feed store.

It seemed weird to have Maggie and the kids with him—weird yet nice.

The faint scent of springtime filled the cab of his truck and alerted his senses to her presence. She wore tan slacks and a black sweater, nothing fancy, yet he couldn't help himself from sliding several glances her way. He noted the depth in her whiskey-colored eyes, the faint sprinkle of freckles across her nose, the allure of her wistful smile as she glanced out the window into the passing landscape that surrounded the Texas community of Winchester.

He wondered what she thought about the place, but didn't ask. She had a small-town simplicity about her, yet there was more to Maggie than met the eye. She was bright and compassionate, driven to perfection. It was best he didn't forget that she'd become a respected physician, that she would leave their new little family after her brief stay in Texas was over.

Jake pulled into the graveled parking lot in front of the feed store and found a space next to the newspaper rack not far from the front door.

"We're here!" Kayla said, as though Jake had just driven to Six Flags Over Texas.

Sam merely whooped his delight.

It made Jake feel as though he ought to take them places more often. The kids always seemed to enjoy going with him, but he didn't have the guts to take them out alone. He usually dragged Rosa along for the ride. But today he had pretty Maggie. For some reason, he felt a lot more comfortable with her at his side.

While Jake helped get Sam out of the car seat, Maggie unbuckled Kayla.

"We're going to see the ducks and chickens, Sam." Kayla smiled at her little brother. "Won't that be fun?"

Sam squealed his agreement, although Jake wasn't sure the kid understood a word Kayla had said.

The Averys, who owned the feed store, usually had animals of one kind or another on the premises, so he didn't warn Kayla that there might not be ducks or chickens. Maybe they'd see rabbits today. Odds were, there would be something to keep the kids happy and occupied.

And today was no exception.

Next to the cash register, a roly-poly puppy napped on a circular pillow. A mutt, probably, but Jake guessed it to have some Australian Shepherd in its bloodlines.

"A puppy," Kayla whispered in reverence. "Oh, isn't it cute?"

"It's absolutely darling," Maggie said. "Look, Sam."

The toddler squatted before the pup and reached out his hand and touched the fluffy black-and-white fur. The puppy yawned and stretched, getting ready, it seemed, to greet his new admirers.

While Maggie and the kids oohed and aahed over the pudgy pup, Jake went about the store looking for the items he'd come to buy. He hadn't gone far when Grant Avery caught him.

Grant had long since handed the financial reins of the business over to his son, but not his vested emotional interest. Each day he came to the store and chatted with customers, sometimes to the point of chewing an ear off. Some folks said he was downright nosy, but Jake figured he was probably just lonely and not ready to throw in the retirement towel.

"Well, hello there, Jake. How're things going?"

"Fine," Jake told the balding, gray-haired man.

"I see you brought the kids along. Who's the good-looking woman?"

"Maggie Templeton." Correcting himself, Jake added, "Doctor Templeton. She's an old friend who came to help out while Rosa's recovering from gall bladder surgery."

"That's nice," Grant said, his gray-blue eyes watching Maggie and the kids. "She gonna stick around after Rosa gets well?"

"Nope. She's going on to California." Jake wasn't up to giving the man too much information. "How're you doing, Grant?"

The old man snorted. "Other than having to grease myself down with arthritis liniment in the evenings, I can't complain."

"Good," Jake said, for lack of anything else to say.

"You ought to get those kids a puppy, son. Look at 'em. All kids need a dog."

"Maybe so," Jake said, although he wasn't sure he

needed another responsibility. He was nearly drowning in obligation already.

"Got that pup from Jim Thompson. You remember Jim, don't you?"

"Yes." Jake remembered the man, a trucker who lived on the outskirts of town.

"His daughter, Diana, moved back home with two young'uns. Too bad about her husband."

At the mention of Diana Thompson, Jake perked up. Although he hadn't seen Diana in years, they'd been friends. Sort of. The kind of old friend a guy thought about every now and again, in a curious, I-wonder-whatever-happened-to-them way.

She'd always had a pleasant air about her. When other girls giggled over a new guy in school or discussed the latest styles, Diana remained low-key and quiet—like she might be hiding secrets of her own. 'Course that might have only been the assumption of a guy who remained on the outside, looking in.

"The poor girl's husband up and died on her, so she came back home for a spell. Seems she used to be a secretary out in Wilmington. I think the last name's Lynch, now. Diana Lynch. Pretty thing, too. And much too young to be a widow."

The old man was right about Diana being pretty. She'd been a head-turner as a teenager, and Jake doubted a few years and two kids had changed that.

Diana had been one of Sharon's friends and one of the few nice girls Jake had actually tried to date before he'd had his fill of Buckaroo Ranch and left on his eighteenth birthday.

She'd sweetly declined his offer, though, and the next fall had gone on to some fancy Bible college in Illinois, where she met and married a minister. "When did she lose her husband?"

"Three months or so," Grant said. "Didn't leave her much in the way of insurance—hardly any medical and no life. Jim Thompson said the Pastor Lynch was okay, as far as preachers went. But he wished his son-in-law would've had a little earthly foresight. Left his family in quite a fix. That's what Jim told me."

"That's too bad."

"It sure is," Grant said. "The church let her stay in the parsonage for a while, but she had to give it up so the new pastor and his family could move in. Poor little gal had to move back home, just so she and those two little girls would have a roof over their head. Now Diana has to find herself a job."

"I'd think her dad would be happy to have her and the kids home, at least until they got their lives sorted out."

"Yep. I suppose he is, but from what I understand, she's determined to move out and get a place of her own."

Jake had to admire Diana for that. Jim Thompson used to be pretty strict and was opinionated to a fault. Maybe the young widow wanted something different for her daughters. "I'm sorry to hear about her husband."

"Yep. Jim told me that his preacher son-in-law used to always say, 'the Lord will provide.' But poor Jim was beginning to think he must be the Lord, 'cause he was always providing his daughter's family with money for one darn thing or another."

No wonder Diana wanted to get out on her own. Her dad's generosity came with a price, or so it seemed. "What kind of work is she looking for?"

"Jim said she was a secretary or bookkeeper or something, but it was only part-time work, and the pay wasn't enough to make a dent in her husband's hospital bills, let alone get them into a new place.''

A secretary or bookkeeper? Jake's thoughts took an interesting turn. He needed someone trustworthy to help out while Rosa was gone. Would Diana be interested?

''Well, now,'' Grant said, nodding toward Maggie, the kids and the puppy. ''Would you look at that?''

Jake smiled as the furry little butterball licked Maggie in the face. It didn't bother her a bit, because she broke into a melodious laugh, one that poured over him like warm brandy sauce over a bowl of bread pudding.

''You might want to give Jim Thompson a call and see if he has any more puppies left. Those kids need a dog.''

Maybe they did. And maybe he should give the Thompsons a call. ''Got a number for Jim?''

''Yeah. Let me look it up.''

While Grant stepped behind the counter, Jake watched Maggie and the kids play with the black-and-white puppy.

What the heck. Maybe he'd surprise them with a dog of their very own. If it put a smile on their faces, it was worth the risk of chewed-up shoes, whines in the middle of the night and accidents on the hardwood floor.

Grant jotted down a telephone number on the back of a business card and handed it to Jake.

''Thanks. Now, if you'll excuse me, Grant, I have some supplies to get.''

And some thinking to do.

An hour after dinner and thirty minutes after bath time, Maggie found Sam asleep in the hallway, a frayed yellow blanket in one hand, a toy police car in the other. The toddler had worn himself out again and, as usual, had lain down on the floor when he'd grown too tired to stay awake.

She picked him up and, unable to help herself, relished his baby-powder scent as she carried him to his crib. Sam was a happy, healthy little boy, full of energy and love.

Just before dinner, he had run up to her in the kitchen, grabbed her leg and squealed in glee. "Mag," he'd said. Then he'd unwrapped his arms and went about his little-boy business. The affectionate gesture had touched her in an unexpected way.

She kissed his chubby cheek, laid him on the bed and tucked him in. Lying in his crib, downy blond hair blessing the mattress, Sam looked like a sleeping cherub.

Warmth settled around her heart. She caressed the top of his head. "Good night, little one."

Maggie stood over Sam and watched him sleep. She wasn't sure how much time she'd spent in his room, but something had rooted her to his bedside. Something peaceful and soothing.

She'd never seen herself as a mother, even though she'd worked with kids for years. The irony didn't escape her, but she usually chose not to think about having a family of her own. Maybe because her own family had been so dysfunctional. Or maybe because she'd carved out a more professional and career-minded life for herself. But a precocious little girl like Kayla and a sweet toddler like Sam almost made her reconsider motherhood.

So precious, so sweet. She whispered a prayer for his slumber, before quietly slipping from the bedroom.

She went in search of Kayla and found the girl sitting under the pink, frilly canopy of her bed, an open book on her lap.

"What story are you reading?" Maggie asked.

Kayla looked up, but she didn't wear the usual grin. Instead, her lips had pursed into a thin line. "Just a book."

"What do you mean, *just a book?*"

The girl sighed, exasperated it seemed. "Just a book I wanted Uncle Jake to read to me, but he said 'not tonight.' That's what he says every time. 'Not now.' 'Not tonight.' Not ever."

Maggie still didn't understand why Jake was so stubborn about taking time to read to Kayla. It wouldn't hurt him to spend five minutes with the child. She'd have to ask him about it—later, when Kayla was asleep.

"He was a fun uncle," Kayla said. "But he's not a good daddy."

Maggie wanted to defend him, but what could she tell the child? That Jake wanted to be a good father to the children, to be a family man, but his insecurities slowed him down and thwarted his efforts? That he feared he wouldn't be a good father because he hadn't had a very good role model? No. She certainly couldn't do that. "Your uncle loves you very much, honey. You're just going to have to give him time to learn how to be a daddy."

"What's so hard about reading stories? Or playing games?"

"Sometimes daddies are too busy to play or read stories," Maggie said. The excuse sounded lame, even to her. Somehow, she'd have to convince Kayla that Jake loved her, even if he didn't do the daddy-type things she expected of him. "Why don't I read to you? It's time for bed, and I want to know what's going to happen next in that story about Professor Bumble."

"Okay," Kayla said.

Maggie took the large, hardbound children's book from the dresser where she'd left it the evening before. "Last night, the professor had just found the keys to the treasure chest. Let's find out what was inside."

Kayla closed the storybook she held in her lap and made room for Maggie on her bed. "I think he's going to find gold and jewels."

"You might be right," Maggie said. "Unless, of course, there's a genie inside."

"Genies live in pretty glass bottles. I think Professor Bumble is going to find a zillion dollars and a pirate's treasure."

"Let's see." Maggie sat next to Kayla and opened the book. She began to read the words aloud, while her mind came to a silent decision.

After story time, and after Kayla drifted off to sleep, Maggie would talk to Jake and intercede on the little girl's behalf.

Surely, she could make him see reason.

And if she couldn't?

Then she'd see how much conflict their friendship could withstand. Maggie didn't mind a challenge, particularly when she went to battle for a good cause.

Chapter Seven

Jake sat in the study, not sure why he continued to stare at ledgers that didn't make much sense. Besides, he didn't feel comfortable behind a desk. Never had; never would.

When he'd first taken over the ranch, he told Rosa that he didn't have time to do the office work. The truth was, he didn't know the first thing about debits and credits and wasn't about to sit through the grueling lessons it would take to learn. The woman did anything he asked of her, including the accounting Jake couldn't do himself.

But Rosa wasn't here, and the paperwork had started to back up. With payday at the end of the week, he needed temporary help. And thanks to Grant Avery's penchant to share the news about town, Jake knew someone looking for a job.

He stared at the phone, wondering what Diana would say about working for a man who still had a bad-boy edge and probably always would. Only one way to find out. He reached into his shirt pocket, pulled out the business card Grant had given him, then picked up the phone and dialed.

Moments later, a familiar voice said, "Hello."

"Diana, it's Jake Meredith."

She paused a moment, and he wondered if she was trying to recall who he was or to figure out why he'd call. "Hi. It's been a long time."

"Yes, it has." Shoot. He'd never been tongue-tied talking to women before. But this call was different. He couldn't skim over her loss. What was a proper response? He didn't know. And now that he had her on the line, he wished he'd given it more thought. "I was sorry to hear about your husband."

"Thank you. It was quite a shock."

Jake figured death always was. "I heard he was a preacher."

"Yes, he was." She paused again. "And it's a comfort to know Peter's in Heaven."

Jake supposed it would be a comfort to her, but he didn't know what else to say, other than another, "I'm sorry."

"You know, Peter spent years telling people that the Lord could call a person home at any time. Funny, but I guess we never really believed the message applied to him or that God would take him at the beginning of his ministry."

Religious talk always made Jake squirm more than emotional stuff, but he wasn't sure how to change the subject.

"It caught us all unaware," Diana said. "My dad is angry that Peter didn't have a life insurance policy for us."

"Well, I'd like to offer you some temporary work at

Buckaroo Ranch, if you're interested.'' He held his breath, awaiting her answer.

She paused momentarily, fueling his anxiety. ''Yes. I'm definitely interested. What do you have in mind?''

''Some office stuff, correspondence, bookwork. It's only temporary, until Rosa Sanchez comes back. But I'll pay you top dollar.''

''Absolutely, Jake. I'd love the job, even if it's only temporary. When do I start?''

Jake looked at the clock on the mantel and smiled. ''Well, I guess this evening's out of the question.''

Diana laughed. ''And so is tomorrow. It's Sunday, and I'm going to take the girls to church. How about first thing Monday morning?''

Jake softly blew out the breath he'd been holding. Thank goodness. Things were finally beginning to look up. His luck, it seemed, had finally turned. ''That sounds perfect to me.''

''Bless you, Jake, you're an answer to my prayers.''

Him? Not hardly. He and God hadn't seen eye-to-eye in years, so it was difficult to think of himself as being an answer to prayer. But if that's the way Diana wanted to see it, then it was okay with him. ''I guess I'll see you the day after tomorrow. But I've got to warn you. The office is a mess.''

''Oh, don't worry about that. If things were in order, you wouldn't need me to work.'' She laughed in a soft, joyful way. ''But don't worry, I'll try to get things under control quickly.''

''Thanks, Diana.''

''By the way, I was sorry to hear about Sharon's death. How have you and the kids been getting along?''

''Fine,'' Jake said, although he figured things could certainly be a lot better. But thoughts of Sam and Kayla reminded him of the second reason he'd called Diana. "Hey, does your dad have anymore puppies left?"

"Yes, four of them. They're really cute. Would you like one?"

"Not particularly," Jake said, with a chuckle. "But the kids would love one. How about picking out a good one for us and bringing it with you on Monday?"

"I'd be happy to. Would you like a male or female?"

"It doesn't matter. Choose one that will make a little girl smile." *And one that will make a pretty doctor smile, too.*

"All right," she said. "I'll see you on Monday morning."

They hung up, and Jake sat back in the leather desk chair and crossed his arms leisurely over his chest.

Yep. Life was beginning to look up.

"Are you busy?" Maggie asked from the doorway.

"Not really," he said, realizing there was more truth to his words than she might believe. He had papers scattered across the desk as though he'd been carefully checking each one, instead of trying to find someone to pass the chore to.

"Can I come in?" Maggie asked.

"Sure. I can use a break."

Maggie wore jeans and a white blouse that had smears of something red and yellow across the front, something that looked suspiciously like ketchup and mustard. The kids had really given her a run for her money today.

Her hair, once combed and neat, was slightly mussed, but it glistened in the lamplight. Any makeup she might have applied that morning had long since worn off, yet there was something downright appealing about the natural blonde standing before him, something that transcended fancy clothes, lipstick and mascara.

He wondered whether she'd scoff if he told her how darn pretty she was.

Probably. Women were weird about things like that. He choked back the compliment instead. He sure as hell didn't want her thinking he was going bonkers over her. He wasn't, of course. But for some crazy reason, he couldn't keep his eyes off her.

The walls of the study seemed to close in on them, reminding Jake of the last time they'd been alone while the kids slept. He could feel her fingertips kneading his shoulders, working his senses. He could still feel her breasts pressed against his back and found the memory arousing by itself.

As he recalled the last kiss they'd shared, he could still feel the heat, the yearning desire Maggie's taste and touch had provoked.

"Care to join me by the fire in the living room?" she asked. "Maybe share a cup of coffee?"

"Sure. Coffee sounds good." Jake scooted the chair away from the desk and stood. The sooner he got out of close quarters, the better. He followed her out of the study, hoping to leave the heated memories behind.

"I'll pour two cups," Maggie said, looking over her shoulder. "Do you still take yours black?"

"Yes." He watched the gentle sway of her hips. "And do you still doctor yours up with cream and sugar?"

"Some things never change," she said with a lilting laugh.

And some things do, Jake realized, as he battled an unwelcome attraction to his old friend and a desire to spend another quiet evening alone with her.

When Maggie returned to the living room, she found a cozy fire in the hearth and the handsome cowboy sitting on the leather sofa, his legs outstretched, an arm draped over the backrest.

Her thoughts took an interesting domestic turn. What would life be like if she were married to Jake? If they tucked in the children together each evening, then curled up on the sofa in front of a fire, savoring a comforting beverage and sharing their day, their hopes for the future?

Silly woman, Maggie scolded herself. She already had a fine future mapped out for herself. And a career-minded game plan that didn't have anything to do with a sexy cowboy or his ranch.

"What did you want to talk about?" he asked.

Thank goodness he put the conversation back on even keel. "I wanted to discuss Kayla."

"What about her?" Jake took the mug she offered him.

Maggie sat on the cushion next to his. She savored a sweet, creamy swallow of coffee before speaking. "I think you should spend more time with her."

Jake blew across the rim of his cup, then took a slow sip. "You're probably right about that, Magpie."

Wow. That was easy. She'd expected him to put up more of an argument. "You know, if you would just read her a story at night—just one—it would please her more than you can imagine."

Jake set the mug on the end table, then raked a hand through his hair, dislodging a dark lock that she was tempted to reach out and brush aside. "Come on, Maggie. Are you going to start on me, too? Maybe it's just a part of my ornery nature, but I don't like being told what to do and how to do it."

Maggie knew all about his rebellious nature. It had gotten him into lots of trouble as a teenager. And probably more so as an adult. "Why are you being so stubborn about something so simple?"

Jake clicked his tongue and sighed. "What if I give her a horse and teach her to ride?"

Maggie brightened. "That would be great. I'm sure she'd be thrilled. It really doesn't matter what you do with her, just as long as you do something special, something that will become a memory someday."

Jake slid her one of those sexy, bad-boy smiles, one that touched her to the core. "I'm glad we found a workable compromise."

"See how easy it is?" Maggie set her mug on the coffee table and gave him an appreciative hug. "Thank you."

She meant the embrace to be an expression of gratitude. Or at least that's what she tried to convince herself. But Jake slipped his arms around her and pulled her close.

Close enough to lose herself in his woodsy scent.

Close enough for her to want more than a hug.

Close enough to bring on unwelcome thoughts of intimacies better left alone.

She loosened her hold, intending to back off and pretend her thoughts hadn't turned sensual, but when he nuzzled her neck, appreciation flew by the wayside.

And desire took its place.

She might be sorry about this later, but she desperately wanted to kiss him again, no matter what the consequences.

Jake was sure Maggie only meant to give him a casual, thanks-for-being-a-friend hug, but he wanted to hold her again.

No. Correction. He *needed* to hold her.

Taking her into his arms, breathing in her faint, springtime scent and feeling her warm, willing embrace only fanned his passion. And he couldn't seem to get enough of her.

He hoped she would make him stop, because he sure as heck didn't seem to have any power over his desire, particularly since whatever good sense he'd once had was gone. He kissed her neck and brushed his lips across her jaw until he found her mouth.

Instead of stopping or pushing him away, she opened for him, allowing him to deepen the kiss and savor the taste of sweetened coffee and cream. He pulled her close and swept his hands along her back, appreciating each gentle curve and fighting the temptation to slip his hands under her blouse and caress her skin.

It might be just plain foolish, but he wanted to lay her down on the sofa and take their friendship a step closer to bed.

Even though they'd both said allowing their friendship to advance to a sexual level wasn't a good idea, Maggie melded into his arms and whimpered while her tongue mated with his. It sure seemed as though she wanted to make love.

But did he?

A growing arousal insisted he did.

Yet he knew a physical relationship often led to emotional intimacy, to the sharing of dreams.

And shortcomings.

That's why Jake preferred to keep his relationships at a distance. He wasn't about to take a chance and pin his hopes and trust on someone he knew was leaving.

Realizing he was venturing close to the point of no return, Jake reluctantly broke the kiss and pulled away. He had to rein in his passion and get it under control, had to regain some kind of hold on his runaway libido.

Maggie, her eyes glazed with arousal, studied him. He wasn't sure what she was looking for. An explanation maybe? Or perhaps the same questions and thoughts he had were raging in her mind, too.

Like it or not, each kiss they'd shared had brought them closer and closer to a full-blown affair.

As badly as he wanted her right now, the thought of making love to Maggie, of broaching that kind of intimacy, scared the liver out of him.

It also excited him beyond belief.

He wasn't sure whether Maggie had changed her mind about the natural progression to a temporary love affair, because that's all their physical relationship could ever be. Could he maintain an emotional distance if their affair only lasted a month or two? He wasn't sure, but a growing desire to have Maggie in his bed suggested he try.

He ran the knuckle side of his hand along her cheek. "How far do you want to take this, Maggie?"

She bit her bottom lip, but he could still see the passion peering from her gaze, the sensual flush to her throat and neck. "This is crazy. I'm sorry I let things get out of hand. Under the circumstances, it's not a good idea. Besides, we've been friends too long to risk ruining what we have."

She was right, of course, but something told him the first day he laid eyes on the very adult, very attractive Dr. Templeton, their friendship had made some monumental change. He nodded in agreement, even though an inner voice laced with testosterone argued otherwise.

"I'll be leaving in a month or so. And where will that leave us?"

Wondering what making love to her would have been like, Jake figured. He raked a hand through his hair, his gaze lingering on the woman next to him. Maggie would soon be on her way and out of his life. So why not admit they wanted each other, why not see where this crazy attraction would take them?

Because Maggie was slowly easing into his home, his family and even his heart—something he couldn't let happen. For her sake. And his.

But if Diana Lynch would work in the office from nine to five, maybe another woman's presence in the house would diffuse the growing sense of intimacy that concerned him.

Then he'd be free to pursue Maggie, at least for as long as she stayed at the ranch. The thought brought a genuine smile and a flood of relief. Maybe he could let a physical relationship develop. Maggie might think that a short-term affair would ruin their friendship, but she seemed to want him as badly as he wanted her.

"When do they need you in California?" he asked.

"Six weeks from now." She offered him a warm smile that reached her eyes. "You know, I'm really looking forward to joining the new pediatric practice, and not just because it gets me away from the embarrassment I faced in Boston. The clinic is affiliated with a prestigious teaching university. The move will be good for my career and another step up for me."

He supposed the move served another, more important need. One Maggie didn't voice, but he knew was under the surface. The respect she would gain in California would also repair the damage done to her self-esteem after that idiot ex-husband of hers had screwed around with the other doctor in her Boston clinic.

"That's great, Maggie. You always were an overachiever. You deserve to benefit from the fruits of your hard work."

"Thanks." Her smile reached her eyes. "And what

about you? Have you given any more thought to what you're going to do with Buckaroo Ranch?''

No. Not when he was so worried about holding things together until Rosa got back. ''I'm always thinking. We'll see what pans out.''

''I'm glad to hear it.''

He shrugged, minimizing his worries. ''By the way, I'm going to hire temporary help in the office.''

''You don't need to hire anyone, Jake. I can do it.''

Jake had a feeling she'd volunteer, but there was no way he'd let her work in the office. It was one thing to grow dependent upon an employee and quite another thing to lean on Maggie any more than he had already. ''You have enough to do, Magpie.''

''But I don't mind. In fact, I have plenty of time when the kids are napping. I'd like to help in any way that I can.''

He paused, as though contemplating her offer, but his mind was made up. ''Thanks anyway, Maggie, but my reason to hire temporary help is twofold. Do you remember Diana Thompson?''

Diana Thompson? Sharon's friend from school? The pretty little brunette Jake had once admitted to having a crush on? Yes, Maggie remembered her.

''Long brown hair that she wore to her waist,'' Jake said, as if Maggie needed the additional reminder, ''with big blue eyes and freckles across her nose.''

Maggie and Sharon had envied the girl who'd developed way before either of them had. Diana had always had a host of teenage boys ogling her, although she didn't appear to notice. She seemed too busy raising her younger brother and running her divorced father's household.

''Diana's husband died, leaving her with two little girls.''

"That's too bad." Maggie had lost her husband, too, in a sense, but death was different. So final. So difficult to explain to grieving children.

"She's come back home and is looking for work. By offering her the job, I can help out an old friend."

An old friend? Had Diana been one of Jake's teenage conquests? Fifteen years ago, she had thought it kind of cute that Jake had a crush on the town sweetheart, especially since she was also a good girl and Jake was a known rebel. It didn't seem so cute anymore.

But who was Maggie to worry about the women Jake found attractive? She quickly shook off the thought and gave him a smile. "I'm looking forward to seeing her again."

And she was. Diana had been a nice girl. And was probably an equally nice woman.

Jake had a wistful look in his eye, one that told Maggie his thoughts had drifted.

She wanted to know in which direction. "You used to like Diana, didn't you?"

"You mean when I was a kid?" Jake chuckled. "She was too decent for the likes of me."

Maybe so, Maggie thought, but opposites attract. And now that Jake had settled down and had a family, he needed a woman who would make a good wife and mother. "Don't sell yourself short, Jake, you deserve the love of a good woman."

He shrugged, then winked at her. "You're a good woman, Magpie. Want to kiss me again?"

Kiss Jake again? No way. She was already too darn tempted to throw caution to the wind and say, who cares about an old friendship anyway? Let's be lovers, just for the next few weeks.

But Maggie was too staid and proper, too goal-oriented for that. Wasn't she?

When Jake had held her in his arms, she hadn't been so sure.

Chapter Eight

After a pancake breakfast on Sunday morning, which Jake didn't stick around to eat, Maggie helped the children choose old play clothes to wear outdoors. The sun burned bright, promising to dry the few damp and muddy spots left.

Maggie dressed Sam in a frayed, blue flannel shirt and worn denim overalls, something she knew could survive a brush with mud and dirt. Kayla put on a gray sweatshirt and jeans. They all went out the back door and into the yard, where a sandbox, playhouse and swing set graced the lawn and grounds.

A redwood table and chair set rested under an elm tree, next to a lawn swing. Maggie thought Sharon might have sat here in the shade to watch her children play. It's what Maggie would have done, had Sam and Kayla been hers.

"I hope my dollies are okay," Kayla said, as she

checked to see how the inside of her playhouse had weathered the storm.

Sam wandered about the yard, until he came to the sandbox. He studied the tarp cover and kicked at it with his foot. Maggie strode across the lawn and raised the black vinyl so he could play.

Carefully lifting his leg, Sam climbed over the wooden frame and plopped down. Several old kitchen utensils lay strewn in the mounds of white sand, along with some other toys, including two small cars and a couple of plastic farm animals. He reached for a little red shovel and yellow rake.

Kayla, who had wandered in and out of the small, gingerbread-style playhouse, wanted to swing, so Maggie helped her into the leather seat. "Hang on, honey."

"I will. Push me, please. I want to go really high. All the way to the sun."

Maggie laughed. "Maybe you should stop when you get as high as the clouds. The sun is pretty hot."

A whippoorwill called from the copse of trees behind the barn. Maggie took a deep breath, relishing the morning air, crisp and clean, thanks to the rain. She closed her eyes and enjoyed the warmth of the sun on her face, the chirp and chatter of birds in the trees, the whinny of a horse in pasture and Sam's giggles of delight.

When had she last enjoyed being outdoors with nothing to do but appreciate the happy sounds of nature and children at play?

"Kay!" Sam bellowed from the sandbox.

"Oops," Kayla said. "Sammy wants me to come help him."

While Maggie slowed the swing to allow Kayla to stop and join her brother, a voice called from the row of rustic-looking cabins that housed the guests in luxury and comfort. "Yoo-hoo! Hello, there."

Maggie saw Vickie walking toward them. She wore skintight jeans, a snug, low-cut sweater and fire-engine-red boots that matched her lipstick.

What did the vixen want? Jake wasn't nearby. At least, not that Maggie knew. She glanced over her shoulder, then scanned the yard. Nope. The cowboy was nowhere in sight.

"I'd like to talk to you," the vixen said.

Maggie tried to keep her eyes from rolling. She couldn't imagine what the woman had on her mind. "Talk to me? About what?"

"I want to apologize for coming on to Jake. I didn't realize you and he were an item."

So the vixen did have a moral or two. That was refreshing. Maggie tried to smile. "No harm done."

Vickie crossed her arms and studied Maggie, as though trying to figure out what a cowboy like Jake saw in her. "You're a lucky woman."

Was she? Even though Maggie and Jake weren't really an item? She didn't feel like a lucky woman, not just in regard to Jake. Luck had little to do with anything in her life. All that she had accomplished, she owed to hard work and dedication. Maggie shrugged her shoulders and attempted another polite smile.

The vixen watched as Kayla made her way toward the sandbox, her steps awkward yet determined. "You know, the first time I noticed the little girl walking like that, I thought she was just playing around. You know, pretending to be a robot or something. What's wrong with her?"

Maggie grimaced. She didn't like when adults, who should know better, discussed a handicapped child as though the kid was a piece of furniture.

Kayla didn't act as though she'd overheard anything, though, and Maggie hoped she hadn't.

Instead of reprimanding Vickie like she wanted to, Maggie answered the question as simply as she could. "Kayla has cerebral palsy, which doesn't seem to slow her down in the least. She's a beautiful little girl and as bright and sweet as they come."

"Well, it's still so sad." The vixen's red-painted lips turned into a frown. "Poor little thing."

Maggie supposed the fact that Vickie was able to feel sympathy for someone other than herself was redeeming, yet at the same time, she didn't want to talk about Kayla like a couple of shoppers comparing the price and quality of tomatoes in the produce section of the grocery store. "Don't feel sorry for Kayla. She's got more strength, character and determination than any child I've ever met. She'll grow up to be and do anything she sets her mind to."

"That's good, I guess." Vickie lifted a bangle laden wrist and swiped at a dark strand of hair that dangled over her eye. She eased closer. "If you don't mind, I'd like to ask you a question."

"What's that?"

"Are you and Jake serious? You know. Getting married?"

Although the query seemed odd, Maggie chalked it up to a lack of social skills on Vickie's part. Should she prolong the act she and Jake had set in motion? She couldn't see any reason to.

The vixen was leaving today. And already packed, most likely. It was nearly eleven, and checkout was at noon.

Besides, last night, she and Jake had decided they were better off as friends. Maggie didn't know how many of those too-darn-hot-for-comfort kisses she could handle.

Under the circumstances, there was no reason to perpetuate the phony affair. "No, we're not getting married. I'm moving to California in a month or two. Jake and I have different lives."

"You don't say." Vickie crossed her arms and shifted her weight to one leg. "I thought, after seeing you two the other night, that there was something going on between you."

For some reason, Maggie wasn't sure what to say. She opted for the truth. "Jake and I are good friends."

"Well," the vixen said, standing taller. "I'd better be going."

Good, Maggie thought. "Have a nice trip home."

"Thanks," the vixen said. "But I've changed my mind about leaving. I'm going to sign on for another week."

The words punched Maggie in the diaphragm. She opened her mouth to speak, but couldn't utter a word, which was probably a good thing. She'd said way too much already and didn't know how to backpedal.

The vixen walked back toward the cabins, her denim-clad hips swaying from side to side as though she had a male audience instead of two disinterested children and a pediatrician with egg on her face.

"I don't like that lady," Kayla said from the sandbox.

Neither did Maggie, but she bit her lip to refrain from venting to the child.

"She doesn't need to talk about me like I'm a nothing," the little girl said. "I don't like it when people do that."

Kayla may have acted as though she hadn't heard Vickie's comments, but she obviously had.

Maggie strode toward the children and sat upon the edge of the wooden sandbox. She stroked Kayla's soft, silky strands of hair. "Sometimes, adults don't think before speaking."

Kayla picked up an old soup ladle and scooped it full of sand. She poured it into a white plastic colander. "Reindeer sure are rude."

Maggie sighed. "Not all reindeer, honey."

Just the red-lipped, air-brained variety.

Maggie blew out a sigh. What would Jake say when he found out that Vickie was signing on for an extra week? Or when he learned that it was Maggie's fault the annoying woman thought he was free for the taking?

Jake came in for lunch, wearing a scowl that would frighten small dogs and children who didn't know him.

"What's wrong?" Maggie asked, while she fished in a sinkful of warm, soapy water for a dishcloth.

"That damn…" He glanced at Kayla, who was munching on a peanut butter and jelly sandwich. "That darn woman is going to stay another week."

Maggie blew out a sigh, as she wrung out the cloth and wiped the countertop of breadcrumbs and a dribble of grape jelly. "That's my fault."

"Your fault? Why?"

She stopped her motions, then faced him with the damp dishcloth in her hands. "I told her that you and I were just friends and that I was moving to California in a month or so."

"Why did you do that?"

"Because it's true." *And because I can't keep kissing you and pretending it isn't having an arousing effect on me.*

"Then tell her you changed your mind, that you want to stay in Texas with me."

Stay in Texas with Jake? Maggie's eyes swept the

kitchen, taking in the sight of Sam in the high chair, peanut butter smeared over his mouth and hair, a banana smooshed in his fingers. His little lips quirked into a smile that touched her heart.

"Yeah," Kayla piped in, looking at her with puppy dog eyes. "You could just stay here. Me and Sam don't want you to go away."

"I'm a doctor, honey. And I have a clinic and patients in California who are waiting for me."

"Can't you be a doctor here? In Winchester? We have to go a long ways whenever we get sick or need a checkup."

"That's because Winchester is too small of a town to support a doctor, especially a pediatrician." Maggie dropped the cloth back into the sink. Her staying in Winchester was out of the question, even if she wanted to, but she didn't suppose the child understood that a doctor didn't just give up the one thing that defined who she was, what she'd achieved, what she had to offer society.

"Yeah," Jake said to his niece. "Maggie can't live in a small town like ours. That would be like asking a superhero to hand over her cape."

For a moment, Maggie wondered whether Jake was poking fun at her ambition, like he sometimes had in the past. But maybe he was just trying to give the child an analogy she could understand. She opted for the analogy and shut down her defensive side. "I've worked very hard to perfect my skills as a doctor, Kayla. Besides, your uncle only wants me to pretend I'm staying in Winchester. And I'm not willing to pretend anymore."

"But what about Vickie?" Jake combed a hand through his hair. "She's been driving me nuts. I'm going to be a sitting target in that annoying woman's scope, just like a lone deer in a meadow."

Maggie laughed, but when she caught the serious glint in his eyes, she realized he wasn't joking. She leaned a hip against the kitchen countertop and crossed her arms. "Come on, you need to be more direct. Simply tell her you're not interested."

"I did, but she doesn't believe me." Jake took a large glass from the cupboard, then opened the freezer door and reached into the ice container. "You don't know how that kind of woman operates."

Maggie had a pretty good idea, although she figured Jake had dealt with quite a few women like Vickie in the past. And watching the handsome cowboy move through the kitchen, she could certainly understand why.

Tall and broad-shouldered, with dark brown hair and blue eyes that sparkled with humor and wit, Jake had more than his rugged, rebel-without-a-cause looks going for him. Add a rough-edged smile that made the heart rate skyrocket and a calloused touch that sent the nerve cells zipping and zapping to the core, and it wasn't difficult to see why he garnered more than his share of female attention.

But a woman like Maggie, who'd had a husband find someone he liked better than her, needed a man she could trust, not a man who had so many female conquests that he'd made kissing an art form. And the fact she found Jake so darn attractive and herself so susceptible to his touch bothered her more than she cared to admit.

Jake poured a glass of tea from the pitcher on the kitchen counter. "Come on, Maggie. You've got to help me out."

"No can do," she said. Her heart couldn't take any more moonlight kisses and late night dreams. "You'll have to figure out another way to avoid her."

"How can I avoid her, when Diana's coming to work

in the office? I can't use bookkeeping as an excuse to duck into the house and avoid her anymore."

"Maybe you can use Diana as a romantic ploy," Maggie said, regretting the words the moment they left her mouth and hung in the air.

Thoughts of Diana and Jake kissing took an odd, tummy-twisting turn, and she didn't want to analyze why. Although, bottom line, she knew what rocked her insides, even though she hated to admit it.

Vickie wasn't the kind of woman a man would seriously consider as a wife and life mate.

Diana was.

"No." Jake took a drink of iced tea, and Maggie watched the muscles of his throat swallow it down. "Diana's not the kind of woman I'd ask to do that."

Maggie didn't know why not, and the fact that she didn't made her uneasy.

"But you don't mind asking me?" Maggie batted at the old insecurities resurfacing and tried to hold them at bay. She tried to laugh, but the sound took on a wry, cynical tone. She hoped he hadn't noticed.

Jake edged close and cupped her cheek. His thumb made a small, circular motion that stilled her laughter and set her senses swirling. His gaze snagged hers and threatened never to let go. "You're my best friend, Magpie."

His hand slowly lowered, and she fought the compulsion to reach for his wrist and hold it in place. Instead, she took a step back.

"You're the best friend I have, too," she said. And she meant it.

But friends didn't make each other go weak in the knees and make them contemplate things best left alone.

By Sunday afternoon, the grounds had dried sufficiently to make Kayla's first ride safe. Jake saddled one of the older, more dependable and surefooted mares and led her from the stable.

Kayla managed an awkward little hop and clapped her hands. "I've always wanted my very own horse. Mommy had promised to teach me to ride, but she never did."

"Well, this is your first lesson. And your very own horse. What do you think?"

Kayla's bright green eyes widened, and her mouth opened in awe. "This is my very own horse?"

"Her name is Sunflower, and she's all yours, if you want her."

"Want her?" Kayla asked. "I love her. And I'll bet she's the best horse in the whole world."

"I'm sure she is," Jake said.

The joy on Kayla's face was contagious, tweaking Jake's heart in a warm, toasty way. He hadn't seen her this happy since before her mother died. He wanted her to stay that way. Forever.

"She's beautiful!" The red-haired girl made her way toward Sunflower and reached to stroke her nose. "I'm Kayla. We're going to be best friends."

Jake didn't doubt her sincerity or the pleasure she'd taken in his gift. He just wished he'd come up with the horse idea sooner. "Would you like me to lift you onto the saddle? We can walk around the corral, just for fun. And if you like her gait and decide to keep her, the lessons will start."

"I'm going to get riding lessons?" Kayla asked.

"Well, sure," Jake told her. "Of course, if you want this horse for your very own, you'll also have to learn how to take care of her."

"All by myself?" Her eyes brightened, and she chewed on her bottom lip.

"Do you need help?"

Kayla shook her head. "Oh, no. I want to do it all. I want Sunflower to be my very own horse."

"Atta girl." Jake lifted the child and placed her on the mare. He adjusted the stirrups to her legs, convinced she was secure in the saddle, particularly on a gentle, slow-poke like Sunflower.

Sharon had always treated Kayla with kid gloves, and several times Jake had tried to get her to loosen up. Once, when he suggested his sister teach Kayla to ride, she'd accused him of being too much like their father—an accusation that sucker punched him. He hadn't made any more child-rearing suggestions after that.

Maggie didn't seem to have any qualms about the girl riding, so Jake assumed he'd been right about his sister. She was a loving mother who was overprotective and way too fussy for a kid's good. Either way, Maggie's lack of concern made him feel better about his offer to give Kayla a safe horse and teach her to ride.

He figured treating her like any other kid was best. Kayla hated being reminded of her disability.

The sun glistened on golden highlights in the child's red strands of hair, giving her an angelic aura. She bent to stroke the mare's neck, then looked up at him with a smile that could light a city block, Las Vegas style. He'd never seen her so happy, and for a brief moment, he wondered if he might be able to parent her after all.

As he led the mare around the corral, he thought about the new puppy Diana was bringing tomorrow. He almost mentioned it to Kayla, but thought better of it. He wanted her to be surprised. And he wanted to see her eyes and smile light up again. It almost made him feel heroic and worthy of her affection. Dadlike in her eyes.

An hour later, Jake had not only walked the corral, but

had also taken Kayla and Sunflower for a walk around the ranch. "Are you getting tired yet?"

"No," the little girl said. "I could ride my horse forever."

Jake laughed. "Well this ol' cowboy is getting blisters. And Sunflower may want a break, too. Tomorrow, when Sam goes down for his nap, I'll start the real riding lessons."

"Real lessons?" she asked.

"That's right." Jake led the horse back toward the barn, while Kayla rode along. "You need to learn about the tack and how to saddle her. Then, of course, you'll learn how to mount and dismount, how to stop and go, turn and back up. And when the lesson is over, you'll need to brush her down and put her back in the stall."

As he helped Kayla down, she wrapped her arms around his neck and nearly squeezed the heart right out of him. "I love you, Uncle Jake. You're the best uncle in the whole wide world."

A knot formed in his throat, and something remarkably similar to tears formed in his eyes. As she released her hold, he had to turn his back, just so the girl didn't see them. He loosely wrapped the reins around the hitching post, even though Sunflower wasn't going anywhere.

"How was the ride?" Maggie asked from the porch. She strode toward them, Sam's little hand held in hers.

Jake was running out of directions to turn, and as Maggie cocked her head and cracked a smile, he realized she'd spotted the emotion brimming in his eyes.

Damn. He hoped she wouldn't comment or expect him to say anything in his own defense. What kind of sappy guy had he turned into?

"Oh, Maggie," Kayla said. "You should have seen

me. You, too, Sammy! And Uncle Jake is going to give me more lessons tomorrow.''

Maggie looked at him like he was some kind of hero, and quite frankly, her pride seemed out of place. He'd done okay with Kayla, outdoors and on his turf. Inside and under the surface was another story.

"Thanks, Jake." Maggie touched his shoulder, reaching, it seemed, for something he'd locked away.

"Can I take Sammy to play on the front porch?" Kayla asked. "He likes to drive his little cars on the furniture. And I'm showing him how to make roads so he can play with the other boys, next time Rosa takes us to play group."

"Sure," Maggie said, as they watched the girl take her brother by the hand and carefully lead him toward the house. Then she turned her attention to Jake. "For a man who doesn't know how to be a father, you sure did a good job of it today."

Jake removed the saddle from Sunflower and tried to ignore the subject Maggie was hell-bent on addressing. "I like working with animals. Teaching Kayla how to ride isn't a chore for me."

"You're a good daddy, Jake." Maggie said. "No matter what you say."

"Yeah, well, this kind of stuff is easy for me."

"It's more than that, Jake. You've always kept people at arm's distance, not wanting to get too close."

So? Hadn't Maggie done the same thing throughout the years? She had her own defensive mechanisms, her own way of avoiding relationships. He didn't see any point in bringing it up, though. He didn't like venturing into that psychobabble stuff.

"Out of love for your niece, you reached out to her,

spent some time with her. And you saw the response you received. That's all she wants—just more of your time."

He hoped that was all Kayla wanted, because he wasn't sure if he could give her anything else. Someday, in the future, he feared he would disappoint her. Let her down. But he wouldn't stew about it. "Like I said, teaching her about horses and riding comes easy."

"It's more than that, Jake. It's reaching out and doing something you're uncomfortable with. I admire you for it." She squeezed his shoulder. "You make me believe in men again."

Her words struck a guilty cord, and he felt himself tense. "I'm not the kind of guy a woman like you should believe in."

Hell, he'd been running from things for so long that, sometimes, it was hard enough to believe in himself.

"Hey," Maggie said, turning him toward her. She wrapped her arms around him and held him tight. "I really appreciate what you did for Kayla."

Didn't Maggie know any other way to thank someone? Jake was no hero, nor was he any of the other things she tried to pin on him. He was just a man—a man who enjoyed the feel of this woman in his arms.

Her flowery scent enveloped him, and Jake closed his eyes. He held her close, enjoying the softness of her breasts against his chest while he caressed the gentle curves of her back and hips.

He and Maggie might both agree that a sexual relationship wasn't in the cards, but for some darn reason, they couldn't keep their hands off each other.

Jake was done trying to postpone the inevitable. He wanted to take Maggie to bed. And he hoped she got over her reservations about having a short-term affair with her best friend, because his own reservations were dissipating by the second.

As her embrace loosened, he lifted her chin, and took her mouth with his.

Chapter Nine

Maggie knew better than to let Jake kiss her again, but she couldn't seem to find the strength or the will to stop him.

Like it or not, his lips worked a gentle magic that touched her soul, and his tongue blazed her core with heat and fire. He pulled her close, flush against an erection that proved the kiss had done something to him, too.

She felt virginal in his arms, inexperienced and new to the thrilling mystery of sex. Jake's kiss awakened a passion in her soul and made her shove all sorts of things aside, logical things like goals and the future, right and wrong.

Did she dare risk having a brief affair with him?

Did she dare not?

His leathery, musky scent pushed her common sense aside, as a slow hand and skillful mouth convinced her she wouldn't be sorry for allowing her body to rule her mind.

Just this once.

She wanted more than his kiss, more than a hint of the foreplay to come. She wanted to make love with him, to lay with him in bed and experience what other women had experienced in his arms.

Other women.

Those old insecurities mounted a full-scale attack and blew a chilling sense of reality back in her face. For years she'd tried to prove her self-worth by being the best in everything she did. Some old habits were hard to break.

Would she measure up?

Did she care if she didn't?

Maggie slowly pushed against his chest, breaking the mind-spinning assault on her rationale.

"You've got to stop doing that to me," she said, her voice husky with the truth of what she'd been fantasizing. She quickly looked to the porch, where Sam and Kayla sat on the wicker loveseat. Kayla held an arm protectively around her brother's shoulder, as Sam drove a little red truck along the bumpy armrest.

"You were a willing participant, Maggie."

Only *too* willing, if the truth were told. She blew out an exasperated sigh. "Okay, I'm obviously attracted to you. I'll admit it."

"Good, because you turn me inside out, lady."

She feared too many women had already turned him inside out, but she was flattered all the same.

"So what are we going to do about it?" she asked.

Jake cracked a knowing grin, his answer clear in the heavy, sexually charged silence.

"And after that? Will once be enough?"

"Maybe," Jake said. "Who knows?"

Maggie sure didn't. But something buried deeply inside, something frilly and romantic and prone to dreams of happily-ever-after whispered that she wanted more than a star-spangled climax. A sexual relationship should mean something other than physical fulfillment. "I don't believe in one-night stands, Jake."

"I'm aware of that, Maggie." He crossed his arms and shot her that bad-boy smile she'd come to expect and, unfortunately, found somewhat endearing. "But I can't offer forever."

And neither could she. A sense of remorse settled over her as she realized nothing would come of their passion and desire, unless one of them crossed the line they'd drawn in the dirt.

Jake glanced at his scuffed boots, then looked up and slid her another smile. "But I've got an idea, a compromise, so to speak. How about a one-on-one relationship until it's time for you to leave?"

Maggie looked at the porch, where Kayla and Sam continued to swing, oblivious to the adult conversation going on and the risk she and Jake would be taking if they let their passion take the lead.

"I don't know," Maggie said. "I need to think about it, Jake."

"Okay. Take all afternoon to think. We can discuss it again tonight."

Maggie's eyes widened, or at least she thought they might have. "I may need more time than that."

Unless he kissed her again, pulled her up against his arousal like he'd done just a few minutes ago.

If that were the case, Maggie wasn't so sure how much thinking she'd do.

* * *

The only light in Maggie's private bathroom was a pair of aromatic candles flickering on the white, wooden shelf near the bubble bath she'd drawn for herself.

She relaxed in the tub, her head resting against the sloped porcelain back, one knee bent and a foot perched upon the waterspout. The soft sound of Beethoven's *Moonlight Sonata* drifted under the closed door.

The kids had gone to bed an hour ago, but rather than stay in the living area and risk running into Jake, Maggie had spent the time alone in her bedroom. Unwilling, she supposed, to give him the opportunity to ask her whether she'd made up her mind about making love to him.

The water, once toasty and inviting, had cooled to luke-warm, and the bubbles crackled and popped.

Time to face the music, so to speak. But she had come up with a tentative decision.

She couldn't risk losing Jake's friendship. And she couldn't risk not being good enough. It's the message her ex-husband had left behind, when he found love in the arms of another woman.

And if there was one thing Maggie couldn't bear, it was not being good enough.

Stupid girl. Can't you do anything right? What were you thinking? The old voices from the past crept into her consciousness, prompting her to chase them away with a slap to the pink-tiled wall that sent puffs of suds floating in the candlelit room.

Would those irrational insecurities ever stay buried?

Maggie rose from the tub and snatched the towel from the rack. As she wiped the sudsy remnants from her skin and dried, she wondered whether making love to Jake might be a good idea after all. Practice, so to speak. So that if and when she ever met another man she wanted to marry, she could have the confidence that she would please him in bed. That she would be good enough. Perfect, in fact.

But she'd never had sex with a man she didn't love. Or care about.

Of course, she loved and cared about Jake. Like a friend.

But friends didn't elicit the kind of feelings that Jake stirred in her. She blew out a sigh. What *did* she feel for him?

Something special. And deep. Frankly, her emotions confused her, but that wasn't so weird. Maggie had always pushed her feelings aside and tried hard to develop her intellect. Her sense of reason.

And whatever she felt for Jake transcended reason. That was for sure.

She grabbed a pair of white panties and stepped into them, then reached for the cotton nightgown she'd laid out to wear and slipped it over her head.

Glancing into the fog-shrouded mirror, she took a quick inventory of her appearance. Her hair, still held up by a big, brass clip, looked all right. She started to reach for her makeup bag, but thought better of it.

She wasn't going to primp for this evening. If the real Maggie Templeton didn't excite Jake, maybe he wouldn't bother to bring up the subject.

And if he did, then maybe she would let the evening play out and see what happened.

Jake sat on the beige leather sofa, his legs stretched out before him, and watched the fire flicker in the hearth. He'd showered and shaved, hoping Maggie would have come to some kind of decision.

A part of him feared the intimacy making love would

bring, but that wasn't the part of him that reacted so strongly to her touch. Her scent. Her kiss.

He'd placed several of Sharon's CDs in the stereo, and the sound of classical music filled the room. Beethoven had seemed more conducive to romance than country and Western, his music of choice.

Maybe Maggie would stay in her room all night, avoiding him and the topic that had lingered in his mind all afternoon.

And maybe that was okay, too.

Jake had a lot of thinking to do. Thinking about Kayla and Sam. About turning the ranch into something other than a fancy Wild West hotel catering to rich people wanting to play cowboy.

He wasn't sure why he looked up and into the arched doorway that led to the back part of the house, but he did. And he spotted Maggie.

She wore her hair up, but several blond strands dangled by her cheek and neck. The skin at her throat and chest was flushed from the bath. A pink robe covered what appeared to be a plain white nightgown. How could a woman dressed so simply, look so darn beautiful and alluring?

He'd had enough women in the past slip into something more comfortable, usually something skimpy or slinky. Their choice of clothing and makeup clearly let him know just what kind of relaxation they were anticipating.

Jake didn't get the same clue from Maggie, but that didn't quell his desire in the least. For some reason, she had the power to turn him every which way but loose, with just her presence, her smile.

"Why don't you sit over here?" he asked, patting the cushion beside him. As she stepped closer, he was drawn to her bare feet and toenails painted the shade of cotton candy and matching her pink robe. He doubted she'd co-ordinated the colors just to catch his eye and entice him, but it worked just the same.

She sat closer to the armrest than to him, and an awkward silence followed. He contemplated how making love would alter their friendship forever. Sex had a way of changing things, especially for him. After a night of loving, and before the sun could rise, Jake naturally began to withdraw from the lady at hand.

As long as the woman didn't expect more from him than he was prepared to give her, it hadn't been a problem. But he wasn't sure what Maggie would expect from him. Or what he could offer her, other than a night of passion neither was likely to forget.

Maybe neither one of them was ready to make that ultimate, no-turning-back decision. Maggie's expression was solemn, as though she'd already made up her mind, but hadn't told him yet.

Did he dread hearing her answer? Or did he still harbor his own fears about getting in too deep with a woman like Maggie? A woman who might set his defense mechanisms into overdrive or break them down, one by one.

He tried his damnedest to shut out her scent, to close his eyes to her simple beauty. To ignore the stirring arousal that her smile could provoke.

The fire licked the logs on the grate in the hearth, casting a warm, cozy glow in the room. Jake glanced at the book-lined wall, taking in each and every spine that reminded him of school, of studying. Of putting his mind to the grindstone and getting something right for a change rather than throwing up his hands and walking away, like he had when high school became too difficult to deal with.

He hadn't ever been sorry for dropping out of school, but sometimes he wished he'd been able to stick it out.

There were a lot of things he wished he'd learned. Like accounting. And parenting, although he figured that was one class he would have bombed for sure.

Rosa saw to all Sam and Kayla's needs, including doctor's visits, which was a great relief to Jake. He'd always felt way out of his league in dealing with kids, particularly one like Kayla. Still, it didn't mean he didn't care or that he wasn't curious about the defect that plagued his niece.

Could he pick the brain of the pretty doctor sitting beside him? Would his lack of understanding show? Or would it seem normal for an uncle to question a physician? Unless he swallowed his pride and asked, he'd never know.

"What caused Kayla's cerebral palsy?"

Maggie turned, surprise evident on her face. The tension he'd first recognized in her features gentled, putting him immediately at ease and making him thankful he'd begun the conversation with a clinical subject far different than the sensual subject he was tempted to broach.

"It's hard to say," Maggie said. "In Kayla's case, I think it was due to her premature birth."

Sharon's pregnancy had been difficult, Jake remembered, although he didn't know all the details. And Kayla had been born too early.

He remembered getting the call, hearing his sister choke on her tears as she explained that she might lose her newborn daughter, the baby she'd dreamed of having. Jake had felt totally out of his element and nervous as hell, but he'd dropped everything and come back to Texas, even though there wasn't a blasted thing he could do, except show his sister he cared enough to be there.

The babies in the nursery had all looked tiny to him. Scary, actually. But when he'd first seen Kayla lying in that little incubator, the other babies seemed huge in comparison. He'd watched as they poked the poor little thing and hooked her up to wires and machines that seemed like bleeping monsters sucking the life out of her, rather than helping her.

He'd cried that day. And he'd prayed, too, for the first time in years. He hadn't expected anyone to actually answer his prayer since it didn't seem like any of his others had ever been heard, but Kayla had lived. And Sharon had been thrilled beyond belief.

Even so, Kayla had been left with a defect he didn't understand. He hoped Maggie wouldn't think he was stupid, but who else could he ask? "Can you tell me more about her disability?"

Maggie drew her feet up onto the sofa and turned to face him. "Cerebral palsy is a general term. It refers to an abnormality of motor control caused by injury to a child's brain during early development."

"You mean before she was born?"

"Yes, but it can also occur during birth, in the newborn period or early childhood."

"Will Kayla get worse?" It was what he feared. When Sharon first told him about the diagnosis, she'd explained that some kids had to use wheelchairs and go to special schools.

"No," Maggie said. "She won't get worse, although she can suffer some complications from the condition. Some children do have more severe cases, but Kayla's diagnosis is mild to moderate."

"Is there anything that can be done to help kids like her?"

"Physical and speech therapies can help reduce the long-term impact." She turned to face him, not actually sliding closer, but closing some of the distance just the same. "There are also support groups, although you'd have quite a drive to find one. It might be easier for you to check online services.''

Online help wouldn't do him a bit of good, since he didn't know squat about computers—yet another subject he'd been curious about. Looks like his best bet was in the city.

''Sharon used to take Kayla into Houston for therapy,'' Jake said. ''Because of the distance, they taught her how to work with her at home.''

''Yes, I know. Sharon mentioned that during one of our last telephone conversations.''

Jake slipped an arm over the back of the sofa, his fingers extended toward Maggie. Her clinical response hadn't diffused his attraction, and in fact had made him want to touch her all the more, but he kept his hand to himself. ''Is there something I should be doing?''

''Maybe. Why don't you make an appointment for a reevaluation with the physical therapist and take her into Houston yourself? If there's more that should be done, they can work with you, like they did for Sharon.''

''That's an idea. I'll call on Monday.''

Maggie reached for his hand and gave it a gentle squeeze. ''I know that I already thanked you for taking time with Kayla today, but I think you made a major step in building a better relationship with her.''

She was right. Today had gone well.

''Kids used to scare me, so I always avoided them whenever possible.'' He shrugged. ''It went better than I expected.''

A smile brightened her expression, erasing all signs of the tension and apprehension he'd seen when she first entered the room and sat down. ''It sounds as though your experience with Kayla was positive for you both.''

She had a point. Jake's talent with animals just might cross over to kids, if he gave it a shot.

Before Sharon had died, she'd belonged to a play group in Janesville, a small town south of Winchester. Rosa had continued taking Kayla and Sam to the park and other events the moms planned for their weekly outings.

Maybe Jake could invite the play group to come to the ranch, offer to give them riding lessons. Then again, maybe not. The idea seemed so far-fetched, even to him, that he was afraid to share the idea with Maggie. Afraid she might encourage him to do something he didn't know anything about, something he really shouldn't try to tackle.

"Today was a good day, I suppose." A slow smile tugged at his lips, and a silly warmth filled his chest. "Did you see how happy she was?"

Maggie gave his hand another squeeze, and he threaded his fingers through hers, wanting the connection, the understanding.

Her smile warmed his soul. "Thank you for spending time with Kayla, for treating her like a little girl, instead of like one of the porcelain dolls on her shelf. I think you'll see some positive changes in your relationship."

"I hope so."

In the growing silence, their gazes locked. Something powerful ignited. Something magical filled the air.

Maggie licked her bottom lip, as though wanting to say something and reconsidering. He doubted she meant to use her tongue in such a sensual way, but it stirred a powerful arousal just the same.

Jake wanted to take her hand, pull her close, press his body to hers, take her to a place she'd never been. Places he'd never been.

But it was Maggie's decision, not his.

He knew exactly what he wanted. Who he wanted. And he had enough experience in making a woman change her mind and become a more-than-willing lover that it would be an easy attempt.

But he wasn't going to seduce Maggie or force her to do something she wasn't ready to do. Even if it damn near killed him to hold back his desire.

Just say the words, Maggie.

She pulled her fingers from his, and he thought she meant to pull away, to tell him their friendship was too special to risk. That what she felt wasn't nearly as powerful as what was rushing through his blood.

Instead, she lightly stroked the length of his forearm, making his hairs stand on end and sending a blaze along his skin. Desire hazed her eyes, announcing a sensual message—loud and clear. She leaned forward, slowly but steadily.

He wanted to close his eyes, feel her nearness, breathe in the springtime fresh scent of bath soap, but his gaze remained riveted upon the passion in her eyes, the softness of her breath.

The anticipation of her touch.

She wrapped her arms around his neck. "Kiss me again, Jake. Convince me that this is right."

Chapter Ten

Maggie had all but made up her mind to never kiss Jake again when his gaze caught hers and locked on to some inner need that touched her heart and sent a heated rush to her core. Desire nearly consumed her.

She wanted to make love to him, more than she'd ever thought possible. She needed to feel his mouth on hers, his hands on her bare skin. And damn the repercussions.

Just this once, she promised herself. Once would be enough.

As she leaned forward to kiss him, he wrapped her in his arms and pulled her forward, claiming her willing mouth with his. Their tongues mated in a wild, primal dance.

A moan formed low in his throat, and her female pride soared, as did her desire. She had the sudden urge to remove her clothes, to feel hot flesh upon flesh, his bare chest against her breasts. She ached to have him inside of her, to have him fill the gaping emptiness that desire had sparked.

Yet a small maternal whisper surfaced, calling a temporary halt to what they'd put in motion. Fighting the tide of passion, she broke the kiss.

"Are you having second thoughts?" he asked, his voice husky, disappointment etched in his expression.

"No. But I don't want to risk the kids wandering out here and finding us."

"Neither do I, even though they're both sound sleepers." He kissed her brow, then slid her a crooked grin. "If you don't mind a change of scenery, I've got a lock on my bedroom door."

Maggie slowly pulled away and got to her feet. She held out her hand. "Then take me to bed."

"There's nothing I'd like more." He stood, then led her down the hall, past the kids' bedrooms and past her own. When they reached his room, he stopped and took her face in both hands. His thumbs, calloused and warm, gently caressed her cheeks. His lips brushed hers with a gentle but urgent kiss. "Are you sure?"

"I'm sure." She scanned his face, the sexually charged intensity of his expression, trying to determine whether he had any reservations. She didn't see any at all. Instead, passion blazed in the blue flame of his eyes, stimulating her in a way his hands and mouth hadn't.

"I'm glad you're sure about this. I want you, too, honey."

Then he drew her past the threshold, closed the door and turned the lock.

As far as she was concerned, there was no going back.

Jake was determined to let Maggie call the shots, at least until it was too late for either of them to change their minds. She couldn't possibly have any idea how hard it was for him to hold himself back, to keep from tearing off her robe and gown and carry her to bed.

But he had every intention of making their lovemaking special, her climax unforgettable.

Maggie strode toward the bed, and he followed her like a lapdog, trying his damnedest to keep the wolf in him at bay. She turned to face him, then slowly untied the sash that held her robe together. She pushed it off her shoulders and let it fall to the floor.

Her nipples pebbled under the thin cotton gown, suggesting her arousal matched his. As she lifted the light cotton fabric that limited his view, he watched the hemline brush past her knees, her thighs. Past the delicate, white lace panties that covered her hips. Past the slim belly he was tempted to smother with kisses. Past small but perfectly formed breasts that fit a man's hand and dusky nipples that begged for equal attention.

She was offering him a gift, one he would cherish, even if he didn't deserve it. He swallowed hard, unsure how much more of the precious view he could take without stroking, kissing. Tasting.

"Maggie," he whispered. His voice held a reverence that surprised him. "You're more beautiful than I could have ever imagined."

"Really?" she asked, as though she hadn't believed him. As though she hadn't ever seen herself in the mirror, or if she had, that she'd never seen herself the way Jake did.

"*Really.*" He slipped off his T-shirt, leaving him wearing only a pair of gray sweatpants. He took her hand and pulled her close, felt her soft breasts splayed against his chest. She melded against him, taunting him to lay her down and throw caution to the wind, to bury himself inside of her and spill his seed.

He placed a hand on her lower back and pushed her hips against his straining erection.

That's when she pulled back.

Oh, no.

Not now.

"What's wrong?" He braced himself for an I-don't-know-what-got-into-me-but-I've-changed-my-mind answer.

The whiskey-brown eyes he found intoxicating grew apprehensive and filled with worry. "Do you have any protection?"

He'd taken a box of condoms from the bathroom and stuck them in the nightstand.

Just in case.

He smiled broadly, then removed a foil packet from the full box in the drawer and held it for her to see. She blew out a sigh of relief. When he'd protected them both, he gave her a lingering kiss that promised more to come.

Joining her on the bed, he loved her with his hands, with his mouth, with his kiss, until she was wild with need.

"Jake," she whispered. "You're driving me crazy. I want you, so bad."

He hovered over her, watching the desire that hazed her eyes, watching the steady rise and fall of her breasts. Wanting to hear her say things neither of them had ever voiced to another.

What had she done to him? What kind of hold on him did pretty Maggie have?

He wasn't sure, but he knew if he didn't plunge into her sweetness soon, he'd die from want of her. Closing his mind to anything other than desire for the woman lying before him, he entered her.

Maggie drew Jake to her, meeting each thrust with her

own, taking and giving in a way she never had. As their desire peaked, a powerful climax rocked her heart and soul. And rocked her world to the very foundation.

For a while, they lay there, wrapped in a cloak of intensity. Maggie was afraid to move, to speak, afraid to break the tenuous connection they'd made.

She wasn't a virgin, wasn't a young woman who'd never experienced the joy and pleasure of sex, but she hadn't anticipated a physical joining to be so utterly heart-spinning, light-shattering and complete.

Jake rolled to the side, taking her with him, holding her close and pulling her into a pleasant afterglow that was every bit as good as the lovemaking they'd shared.

Once would be enough, she'd told herself. But now she wasn't so sure. How could someone make love like that and never want to do it again?

Jake brushed his lips across her brow and pushed a strand of hair from her eye. "I hope you don't have any plans for the rest of the night."

Maggie stroked his cheek. "And what if I do?"

He gave her a long, deep kiss. "Then I'll have to convince you to stay with me for a while longer."

Maggie slid him a crooked grin. "Give it your best shot, cowboy."

Jake laughed, then began to work his magic all over again.

The morning sun peeked through the curtain, waking Maggie with a warm slice of sunlight in her eyes.

The scent of lovemaking lingered on the sheets, along with Jake's musky cologne. The only thing that didn't linger was the handsome cowboy who had turned her senses inside out and showed her things about her body she hadn't known or studied in a textbook.

She sat up in bed, pulling the sheet to cover her breasts, and scanned the bedroom. A pair of jeans hung over the back of a leather-upholstered easy chair. A Navajo rug hung on one wall and a dark oak dresser and mirror graced the other. A few piles of male clutter dotted the bedroom, staking a claim and calling it his own.

The clothes he'd been wearing last night were no longer on the floor, where he'd hastily left them.

And neither were hers.

The robe and gown now lay across the foot of the bed. An indication of his thoughtfulness? Or an invitation for her to put them on and leave his room? She wasn't quite sure.

The nightstand drawer that held the box of condoms that had come in so handy last night was closed, leaving little evidence of their lovemaking.

Maggie flopped back in bed and flung an arm across her eyes. What had they done?

And what would the repercussions be?

She fell into the midst of the proverbial morning-after, with thoughts of *now what?* echoing in her ears.

Was she sorry?

Not exactly. But she did suffer a pang of regret that their lovemaking wouldn't lead to something better and deeper. Something lasting. Of course, that was impossible. She would head to California in less than two months, where she would immerse herself in her work, as she always did.

Maggie Templeton thrived on her career, in her practice, offering her patients and their parents something other pediatricians sometimes couldn't.

The affair she'd entered into with Jake would—could—only be a fling. Something to bolster her pride until she got elbow-deep into her new medical practice. Yet the

aftereffects of her actions kept bombarding her conscience
in the form of questions that had no apparent answers.

Was Jake sorry for what they'd done, what they'd
shared?

She doubted it. Men, and Jake probably in particular,
loved sex for the physical release it brought. Women, like
her, usually wanted more from a relationship. She shoved
aside weak, irrational thoughts of ever-after and reiterated
her need for a no-strings-attached physical release, too.

Had she measured up to Jake's other lovers?

She had no idea and wouldn't be able to guess until
she'd faced him and tried to read his expression.

Maggie shook off her worries and kicked off the covers.
Maybe she'd feel better once she'd showered and dressed.
But first she took time to make the bed they'd rumpled
so thoroughly the night before. A part of her hoped she'd
left a trace of her scent, a memory for him to keep.

She didn't bother putting on her gown, but slipped into
the robe and stole down the hall. Stopping in the doorway
of each child's bedroom, she took a quick peek and found
Sam and Kayla still asleep. Thank goodness.

She'd have time to shower and put herself together. No
one would be the wiser.

Except her.

And Jake.

Dumb girl. Stupid girl. The voices came back, ques-
tioning her decision, but she pushed them aside and turned
on the shower spigot. When the water produced steam,
she tested and adjusted the temperature, then slipped off
her robe and stepped under the soothing spray, willing her
worries and irrational concern to funnel down the drain
along with the soap and suds.

What's done is done, she told herself. Besides, she'd
be leaving Texas soon enough.

But could she pack up and drive away, knowing she might never again experience lying in Jake's arms?

She would have to.

Dr. Maggie Templeton had a professional duty to fulfill in California.

Jake had awakened before dawn to find Maggie tucked neatly in his arms, her back to his chest, his hand resting protectively on her hip. It was a sleeping position he could easily get used to, at least until she moved on with her life. Making love to Maggie had been better than he could have imagined, but the future of their affair, no matter how brief, was in her hands.

In the past, with lovers who'd grown too possessive, too clingy during the night, he would often slip off without waking the woman sleeping next to him and leave before she could ask for more than he was willing to give.

This morning he hadn't felt that overwhelming sense of escape that had plagued him before, but past experience allowed him to slowly ease away from Maggie, to climb from bed while she still slumbered unaware.

But this time, his reasons for quietly leaving the room were far more complex.

He'd wanted to let her sleep. To let her think about the future, what little of it they had together. And while she did that, he'd face the reality of morning and the pitter-patter of little feet. He also wanted the household settled and running smoothly before Diana arrived at the ranch. As soon as he showed her the office, he planned to disappear for the rest of the day.

The plumbing snorted and rumbled, announcing someone had turned on the shower down the hall. Maggie, no doubt, was awake. And it would be only minutes before Kayla and Sam began to stir.

Jake filled the coffeepot with water, then reached into the canister by the sink, scooped out heaps of freshly ground coffee and placed it in the filter. He and Maggie could talk about the future later this evening, when the kids were asleep. Maybe he'd take her outside on the porch, enjoy the sounds of a Texas night and catch sight of the moon as it peered through a dark, cloudy sky, sit on the lawn swing and hold hands.

Moonlight and lawn swings?

Sheesh. He was getting too damn sappy for his own good. A midnight ride with a couple of long necks and a sleeping bag to lay under the stars was more his style. But having kids underfoot had changed his game plans for good, so it seemed.

The coffeepot began to gurgle, just as Sam called for his sister. The kids would soon wander into the kitchen, looking for breakfast. Jake didn't have time to fuss with bacon and eggs. Juice and cereal would have to do.

Sunlight filtered through the window over the sink, bathing the room in natural morning light. Before the coffee had finished brewing, Jake poured himself a mug, then quickly slipped the pot back in place.

He wondered when he could expect Diana. They hadn't discussed a particular time, but he hoped she was an early riser. The minute she stepped through the front door, he was ready to lead her into the office and let her solve the bulk of his bookkeeping problems.

Buckaroo Ranch ran smoothly, without much of his involvement, thanks to the dependable employees his uncle and sister had hired over the years. But payday was fast approaching, and if the checks weren't handed out on time, there'd be plenty of grumbling in the ranks—something he didn't want to risk.

Jake took a sip of hot coffee and savored the deep, rich

flavor of an especially strong brew, just as he liked it—loaded with enough caffeine to jump-start his day. He and Maggie hadn't gotten much sleep last night.

Not that he was complaining. A slow grin crept onto his face. Their lovemaking had gone into overtime, and if he hadn't been responsible for his niece and nephew, he would have stayed in bed for another marathon session starting at the break of dawn.

"Good morning," Kayla said, as she led her little brother into the kitchen. "Is breakfast ready?"

"Almost. How about a glass of juice?"

"Okay." Kayla still wore a pink-and-white nightgown that bore a unicorn on the front. Sam, on the other hand, wore only a plain blue pajama top. He'd lost his bottoms somewhere along the way. A diaper appearing new and dry sagged to the point of being worthless if nature called.

Kayla grinned from ear to ear. "I changed Sam's pants, all by myself."

Jake was glad to hear it. Changing wet, overloaded diapers was one nasty job he'd never get used to. "Thanks, honey. I owe you, big time."

"And I washed my hands, too." Kayla beamed, her pride apparent.

"Atta girl. I sure appreciate your help." Jake wondered if the improvement in their relationship had caused this new attitude and grown-up response. Probably. He kicked himself again for not giving her that horse sooner.

The plumbing squawked again as the water stopped rushing through the pipes. Maggie had probably climbed from the shower and was drying off. What was she thinking? That what they'd shared had been good?

Good? It had been great. And even though he couldn't imagine how two lovers could improve something damn near perfect, Jake had a feeling this evening might prove even more pleasurable than last night.

He lifted Sam into the high chair. "There you go, kiddo. Want some OJ?"

"Duice," the towheaded toddler said.

Hoping to prompt a "please" like Rosa always did, Jake asked, "What do you say?"

Sam lurched in his seat and stretched out his chubby little hands. "Pees."

Glad the kid was finally learning to communicate, Jake poured orange juice into one of the small, spill-resistant cups with two handles and gave it to the little boy. "Be careful, pal. I don't have time to clean up after you this morning, and I don't want to dump that chore on Maggie."

Not this morning, anyway. He wanted her to enjoy the escape from reality for a little while longer, to think about their lovemaking and dream about the night to come.

Before he could get Kayla something to drink, a knock sounded at the back door. He had already assigned most of the guest ranch duties to Earl Iverson and Billy Ray Backus, two men who'd worked on the ranch for as long as he could remember. They were competent, so hopefully they had everything under control and only wanted to run something past him.

If this were a working ranch that belonged to Jake heart and soul, things would be different. He would thrive on personal involvement, not wanting to delegate responsibility to anyone else.

But things weren't different.

When he opened the door, he found Diana on the service porch. She'd changed, he realized, but in a grown-up, motherly sort of way. She wore a pair of black slacks and a gray sweater. Her chestnut-brown hair, once long and to the waist, bobbed just below her ears in a pixie cut. It suited her, he decided. "Boy, am I glad to see you."

"Thanks. I didn't know if I should use the front door or not. Sharon used to bring me in this way." She fidgeted with the thin shoulder strap of her purse.

"The back door is fine. Come on in." Jake stepped aside and shot her a welcoming smile. He'd told her bright and early Monday morning. Apparently, she was just as eager to get busy as he was to hand over the keys to the office.

"We didn't decide on a specific time, and I didn't want to be late," Diana said. "I hope I'm not too early."

"You're just in time, especially if you want a cup of coffee before getting to work."

"Coffee sounds great." She entered the kitchen, her gaze resting on the children waiting for breakfast.

"Kayla, this is Mrs...." Jake paused, forgetting her married name.

"Mrs. Lynch," she supplied. "But you can call me Diana. I'm glad to meet you Kayla. Your mommy and I used to be friends."

"Like Maggie?" Kayla asked.

Diana glanced at Jake.

"Maggie Templeton is in town. She came out to watch the kids while Rosa is recovering from surgery."

"Oh, I remember her. She's the friend of Sharon's who stayed summers here. That's really nice that she could come help." Diana said, before returning her attention to the child. "How old are you, Kayla? Should I guess?"

Kayla nodded, her grin sporting two dimples.

"Let's see." Diana, clearly comfortable with children, studied Kayla with a thoughtful assessment. "Maybe five. Or six?"

"I'm five," Kayla said proudly. "And you're good at guessing."

"Well, I have a little girl about your age. Her name is Jessica."

"Why didn't you bring her?" Kayla asked. "I could show her my playhouse and swing set."

"Someday, I will. But today I came to help your uncle work in the office."

Kayla nodded sagely, drawing a smile from Jake.

"Oh," Diana said, as though suddenly remembering something. "I brought the little item you requested, but left it in the car." She nodded outside, indicating he should know all about it.

The puppy.

He'd nearly forgotten. But before he could comment, Sam squealed with glee. "Mag!"

Jake glanced in the doorway, where Maggie stood wearing faded blue jeans and a crisp white blouse. Their eyes met, and memories of their night of passion flashed between them, pulling them from the crowded kitchen and depositing them in some small universe of their own.

"Hi, Maggie," Diana said, stepping forward and beaming them back to earth. "It's good to see you again."

Maggie smiled awkwardly as though Diana's presence had surprised her.

Or bothered her, maybe. Was she worried that Diana could sense what pleasures Maggie and Jake had shared throughout the night? Or was she thinking about something else?

Hell, what did it matter? Men were usually way off base when they tried to figure out what a woman was thinking.

Still, Jake figured he should say something, but before he could utter anything clever to disperse the awkward moment, Sam let loose a little rebel yell, and in his excitement, the plastic glass flew across the kitchen, sending a rain of orange juice through the room, most of it landing on Maggie.

Her jaw dropped to the floor, and she looked first at Diana, then turned to Jake.

The shy, inept expression she wore was one he hadn't seen in years.

Chapter Eleven

Maggie hadn't expected to see Diana so early in the morning or to find her chatting with Jake and the kids in the kitchen.

And she certainly hadn't expected Sam to screech with delight and sling a full glass of orange juice at her. Whether he'd thrown the cup or flung his arm and batted it across the room was anyone's guess, but the chill of the juice seeped through her bra and onto her breasts.

She glanced down at the large, pulp-riddled splotch on the white blouse she'd pressed yesterday afternoon. Before she could move, Diana had grabbed the dishcloth from the sink and brought it to her.

"I guess Sam was a little excited to see you," Diana said. "You'd better get that rinsed out before the stain sets."

Maggie quickly recovered, donning her professional

stance and smiling at the pretty woman with cornflower-blue eyes and a gentle smile. "Thanks."

Diana took some paper towels from the roll and cleaned small splatters of juice from the wall and floor. The task wouldn't be too daunting, since most of it had landed on Maggie.

"Ah, Sammy." Jake grabbed a wad of paper towels and wiped the toddler's hands. "Don't throw things in the house. Look at the mess, buddy."

Maggie tugged at the cold, wet cotton that clung to her skin, but it didn't help. Diana was right, she'd have to soak her blouse and put on something else.

"Hey, kids," Jake said, as he tossed the soiled paper into the trash. "I've got a surprise for you."

"A surprise?" Kayla's eyes widened. "What kind of surprise?"

"Let's walk outside and see."

Sam didn't seem to understand why he was being removed from the high chair, but caught up in Kayla's excitement, he shrieked and toddled outside. His diaper hung haphazardly on one side. Maggie feared the darn thing would fall off before he made it to the front yard.

She appreciated the fact that Jake changed the boy's pants, but he certainly could have done a more secure job of attaching the adhesive strips to the side. He was right about one thing—he didn't know anything about taking care of children.

But he was trying, and she had to give him credit for that. A lot of credit. Watching the tough guy loosen up around the kids touched her in a way she hadn't expected, filling her heart and making her smile.

As they walked in the bright sunlight, Maggie wondered where Diana and Jake were leading them. To the parking lot? That's where they seemed to be heading.

They stopped in front of an old, olive-green Plymouth that hadn't been parked in a garage for ages. Years of dust and heat, rain and ice had battered the drab exterior. The wheels had no hubcaps, and the tire treads were, if Maggie guessed correctly, just barely within legal safety limits.

Diana opened the door and reached across a worn, blue-and-green-striped towel that covered the driver's seat. She pulled out a roly-poly puppy that looked like the one they'd seen at the feed store.

Kayla stood mesmerized, eyes wide and mouth agape. Sam waddled forward and, on tiptoes, managed to stroke the little black-and-white tail.

"Mr. Avery's puppy," Kayla uttered.

"No," Diana said, handing the pup to Jake. "This one is his sister."

Jake carried the little ball of fur toward Kayla and stooped for her to see. "I thought that you and Sam might like a dog of your own."

"A dog of our own?" Kayla's surprise blazed on her face, tweaking Maggie's heart again. What a sweet, thoughtful thing for Jake to do.

Still kneeling before his niece, Jake glanced up at Maggie, catching her eye. Something soft and gentle passed between them. Something warm and fuzzy that pulled her into the family circle.

A circle she had no business joining.

Using the wet blouse as an excuse, Maggie left the children with the puppy, Jake and Diana. As she trudged back to the house to change her clothes, the puppy made a little half growl and half bark noise.

A melodious blend of adult and child laughter followed, but Maggie continued her trek without looking back.

* * *

Jake rode the perimeter of the ranch, checking fence, he told Billy Ray. But the truth was, he wanted time alone, time to remember what life used to be like when he could come and go as he pleased, footloose and fancy-free. Time to remember the life he'd led before becoming strapped with Buckaroo Ranch.

A blue jay called from the copse of cottonwoods that grew by the lake and along the creek. Jake urged his mount toward the swimming hole where he spent much of his free time as a teenager.

To the west, Earl led a group of guests along the trail, taking them back to the ranch. The old man waved, and Jake gave him a nod in recognition. Thank goodness he didn't have to take folks on those boring rides, following the same dusty path day in and day out.

Years ago, before his mom died and his dad took to drowning his sorrows in hard liquor, the family had taken a trip to Southern California and stopped at Disneyland. The miniature cars in Tomorrowland had caught Jake's young eye, and he'd stood in line for what seemed like forever, just to get his turn. When he finally slid into the driver's seat, he realized the steering wheel did little more than give a kid the feeling he was really driving. Those cars didn't go anywhere, other than the prelaid track.

And neither did those Buckaroo horses.

Who could live like that? Plugging along on the same trail, day after day. He couldn't, yet that's what fate had saddled him with.

Jake pulled up when he reached the swimming hole. He scanned the oak trees that rimmed the grassy shore. Would Kayla like it if he brought her here, if they packed a picnic lunch and came out to play in the water? Maybe so. Funny, how he wanted to see her smile again in that happy, little-girl way.

She might even put her arms around his neck and squeeze it tight. Tell him she loved him and that he was the best uncle in the whole world.

He wasn't, of course. But it sure felt good to hear her say it.

The old rope still hung from the limb on which he'd tied it years ago. The rope he used to swing from every chance he got. It might have yellowed and frayed over the years, but the memories of the fun had not.

Jake had brought Maggie out here many times, where they swam and laughed in the summer sun. Sometimes they skipped stones across the water's lazy surface, while talking about the hand life had dealt them and what they both intended to do about it. And other times, they would lay on the grassy slopes with fingers clasped under their heads, watching clouds and just being friends.

One especially hot and humid August day, Jake had talked himself nearly blue in the face, but he'd finally managed to get Maggie to climb the old, gnarly oak tree, take hold of the rope and swing Tarzan-style across the lake. He'd had to glide with her, of course, and drop into the cool lake water while holding her hand.

Would she be easier to convince now? Not likely. But he figured it'd be fun to suggest. He felt the rise of a slow grin. Maybe he ought to replace that old rope with a new one that was strong enough to support the weight of two adults.

In fact, if Rosa came back to work before Maggie left, he'd have the older woman baby-sit one night so that he and Maggie could slip out here and make love under the stars. That was a memory he'd like to make, and one that he'd keep, long after she'd gone.

"Yoo-hoo," a familiar voice called from the trees.

Oh, brother. Not her again.

Jake looked over his shoulder, and sure enough, Vickie and her mount had wandered away from the Stepford horses. Most of the guests wore Western wear on their ride, but not Vickie. She wore a formfitting sweater that was cut too damn low in the front. He guessed she had on one of those push-up bras that shoved her breasts front and center.

"I haven't seen you around lately, Jake." She arched back in her seat, as though stretching out from a long, hard ride, but he figured she was just showing off her wares.

He wasn't window-shopping.

She licked her lips, in a slow, sensuous way. "Lately, you've been so busy that I haven't hardly seen you around."

"I've got a lot of responsibilities."

"It looks like you've got some free time now," the woman said with a Mae West smile. "So I'm going to be direct."

Jake blew out a heavy sigh. Vickie was going to be *more* direct? He doubted that was possible.

"I'd like to spend some private time with you, alone and in my room. Time's ticking away, and you haven't had a chance to test my bed springs."

He'd show her direct, just like Maggie had suggested. "Listen, Vickie. You're barking up the wrong tree. I'm not interested in having a relationship with you. You're not my type."

She leaned forward in the saddle and giving him a bird's-eye view of breasts that threatened to spill out of the low-cut, cherry-red knit. "What kind of woman do you want me to be?"

"A woman like Maggie," he said, without giving it any thought.

Vickie sat upright. "I thought she was your friend. And that she was moving away."

"Yes, but we have a commitment until that time comes." He'd spent the bulk of his adult years avoiding even a hint of permanence in a relationship, but the word slipped easily out of his mouth, surprising him.

But they *did* have a commitment, at least until she left for California. And for once, it didn't bother him in the least to be bound to one woman, especially if that woman was Maggie. "Come on, Vickie. Let's head back to the ranch. Dinner will be ready soon, and I want time to clean up."

Besides, he had been daydreaming about nighttime activities long enough.

After the sun set and the kids had been tucked into bed, he planned to spend a quiet evening in Maggie's arms.

Maggie spent most of the day chasing after Sam and the little black-and-white puppy Kayla had aptly named Oreo. The pup was a cute little thing and appeared to love the children as much as they adored it.

During intermittent moments of free time, Maggie tackled the laundry, washing and drying, folding and putting away. Several times during the morning, while taking an armload of clean clothes down the hall, she passed the open office door, only to see Diana working diligently, not even taking time for a lunch break.

Around midafternoon, the new bookkeeper worked on a pile of invoices. A brown bag rested on the desk, and she munched on slices of apple and cheese. Maggie wasn't sure how much she'd actually accomplished, but by the time the ornate grandfather clock struck five, the desk was tidy and neat, with only a stack of checks awaiting Jake's signature.

Diana and Maggie walked to the front door and chatted about a few inconsequential things, about weather, children, puppies and the like. Then they said goodbye, and Diana left for the day. Or so they both thought.

The tired-out Plymouth had other ideas.

Diana returned to the house with the hope that a simple jump start would solve her problems. According to Billy Ray, Jake was still out riding the fence, but due home any minute, so Maggie suggested they wait on the porch.

While the puppy slept on the wooden flooring and the children hovered nearby, anxious for playtime to commence, she and Diana relaxed in padded wicker chairs, drinking glasses of iced tea. They watched the sun dip low in the sky and caught up on the past—something Maggie surmised that they both enjoyed.

"We shouldn't have to wait much longer for Jake," Maggie said. The last afternoon trail ride had ended, the saddle-sore guests had gone to their rooms to freshen up for dinner and the ranch hands were busy putting away the horses.

"I hope he can get my car started," Diana said. "I know it's on its last legs, but it's the only transportation I have."

Diana hadn't gone into detail, other than to say that her minister husband had passed away and that money was scarce. Maggie had a feeling the financial trouble started long before Pastor Lynch died, but she kept her thoughts to herself.

"Can't we please wake Oreo up?" Kayla pleaded a second time in a matter of minutes. "She's been resting long enough."

"No," Maggie said, "not yet. That poor little dog is still a baby, and she's worn-out."

Kayla blew out a disappointed sigh. "How many more minutes does she need to nap?"

Sam clutched his tattered yellow blanket, stroking the frayed satin edge while sucking his thumb. Obviously, Oreo wasn't the only baby exhausted from hours of play-time.

Maggie looked at her wristwatch. "Five more minutes, at least."

Diana scanned the horizon. "I hope Jake gets here soon. My dad has a long haul this evening, and he's probably awake and ready to go. My brother's going to night school and has a class tonight. I've got to get home before he has to leave the house." She blew out a weary sigh. "I hate to be so troublesome and on my first day, too."

"You're not any trouble," Maggie said. "I can give you a ride home, then you can worry about the car later."

"If Jake doesn't get here in the next few minutes, I may have to take you up on the offer." Diana placed her glass upon the wooden patio table. "I'm really sorry about this."

"Don't worry about it. I'm not used to being tied to a house all day. It will be nice to take a drive."

Diana attempted a grateful smile, but it failed to reach her eyes. "I probably shouldn't have taken this job, since I haven't lined up a permanent sitter to watch the girls after school and I can't depend upon that car to get me back and forth to work. It's just that I've got to get back on my feet before..." She paused.

Maggie wondered whether she was carefully choosing her next words or trying to take the last ones back. "You have to get back on your feet before what?"

Diana leaned back in the chair and rested her hands in her lap. "Before my father browbeats the kids like he did my brother and me."

"Is he abusive?" Maggie asked, the physician in her stepping to the forefront. She'd had to deal with more than her share of child abuse and domestic violence cases and knew many went unreported.

"He's not abusive in a physical sense. But he snaps and growls so much that he sure does a number on a kid's self-esteem." Diana cast a sorrowful gaze at Maggie, bearing testimony to memories that had become more taxing than most people might guess. "My mom ran off when I was six years old. I don't know the details, but I've always believed she couldn't take his criticism anymore."

"Emotional abuse can sometimes be more damaging than physical abuse."

"Don't get me wrong," Diana said. "My dad loves me and the girls. He'd do anything for us and he does. He works two jobs and would give us the proverbial shirt off his back. But he has such a miserable side to him. A grumbling, unhappy, critical way of looking at life and those around him." She clicked her tongue. "My grandpa was a drill sergeant, and from what I understand, my dad took a lot of verbal abuse as a kid, too."

"You'd think that most kids who'd grown up in abusive families would break free of the cycle and create a loving environment for their own children," Maggie said. "Or that kids who'd grown up while living with an alcoholic wouldn't subject their own children to that kind of life. A few break free, but patterns are hard to break, without a determined and conscious effort. I'm glad you want something different for your daughters."

"I guess that's why I married a minister. I wanted someone gentle and loving. Easygoing."

Maggie merely nodded. She'd never given marriage and family that much thought. Her plans had always been to better herself, something she was constantly doing. She had never focused on hearth and home.

Diana let out a sarcastic little laugh. "But you know the old adage, 'Be careful what you pray for, you just might get it.' I just went from one extreme to another. Believe me, I'm going to think long and hard before I ever get involved with another man again."

Maggie wasn't exactly sure what Diana meant, but before Maggie could comment, Jake rode into view.

And so did Vickie.

What were they doing riding together?

Alone.

Had Vickie talked him into one of those private, romantic rides?

That's enough, Maggie scolded herself. Everyone knew the vixen followed Jake around like a star-eyed groupie. And he wasn't interested in her. Besides, he and Maggie had a commitment of sorts.

Would her ex-husband's betrayal cause her to question the honesty of every man she became involved with? Not if she refused to let it. Not if she made the conscious decision to trust Jake.

It was the right thing to do; the only thing to do. Maggie sat back in her seat and relaxed, as Jake helped the vixen from the saddle.

This time the woman didn't fawn all over him. Instead, she thanked him and handed over the reins of her buckskin mount, then walked back to the cabin she'd been assigned.

Diana stood. "Well, I guess I'd better tell him about the car. I hope it's just the battery. Maybe he can jump-start it, and I can be on my way. Thanks for the tea."

"You're welcome."

"What's up?" Jake asked.

Diana made her way toward him. "I'm sorry to dump my problems on you, but my car won't start."

Jake adjusted the Stetson riding easily on his head. "Let me hand these horses over to the stable boys, and I'll take a look. But I've got to warn you, my expertise is with animals, not engines."

"I really think it's the battery," Diana said. "My dad changed the oil yesterday and said everything looked as good as could be expected. He didn't think I'd have any trouble with it for the time being."

"Well, I'll take a look. If it's more than a bad battery, we may need to wait on some parts."

Diana sighed. "If it's more than that, I may have to trouble you guys for a ride home. My dad has probably left already, and my brother will be leaving for night school soon. I don't have anyone to look after the girls."

"Then we'll hope a simple jump start will work. If it doesn't, I'll take you home." Jake glanced at Maggie. "You don't mind holding dinner for me, do you?"

"Not at all," Maggie said, trying to quell a little quiver in her stomach.

As Jake led the horses into the barn, Diana joined Maggie on the porch. "Jake may have had a bad reputation as a teenager, but he really is a nice guy."

Yes, Jake was a nice guy. Much nicer than folks in town had given him credit for. Was he the kind of guy who balanced the extremes of a critical trucker and a mild-mannered minister?

An unwelcome sense of something akin to jealousy sprang from her chest, which was highly unusual and totally unacceptable behavior for an educated professional.

Besides, Maggie didn't have a jealous bone in her body.

Yet a small, green-eyed voice whispered otherwise.

Get a grip, she told herself. She had no claim on Jake,

other than for the next month or two. After that, they had two separate lives to lead. Jake deserved to find a loving, kindhearted woman who could be a helpmate, a woman who would be good to the kids. A woman with whom he could build a home.

A woman like Diana, the green-eyed voice whispered.

Enough of that. Jealousy didn't become Maggie. She wasn't a suspicious, possessive, emotionally needy type. She was a dedicated professional, and it was best she remembered that. Garnering all of her self-control, Maggie shoved those irrational insecurities as far from her mind as possible.

From this moment on, she would make a determined and concentrated effort to rid herself of patterns unbecoming of a respected physician.

She would forget about jealousy, Jake and impossible dreams that would never amount to anything of significance.

Chapter Twelve

Jake disconnected the jumper cables and put them behind the rear seat of his pickup. A dead battery was the least of Diana's troubles.

The odometer of that thirty-year-old Plymouth had lapped more times than a veteran stockcar driver and still boasted more miles than a frequent flyer. If the car had been a horse, it would have been put out to pasture years ago.

Jake placed a hand on her small shoulder and guided her toward the passenger side of his truck. "I'm sorry, Diana. Looks like I'll have to give you a lift."

She looked up at him with tired eyes, the kind that said it wouldn't take much more to bring on a gush of tears. "I'm probably falling all over myself apologizing, but you have no idea how badly I feel about this."

He always steered clear of emotional women, but he sensed that this one had a legitimate reason to cry. "I've got to run into town anyway," he said, even though he really didn't. "Don't give it another thought."

She allowed him to open the door for her, then climbed inside and waited until he slid into the driver's seat. When he did, she offered him a small but appreciative smile. "Okay, but you won't have to take me home again. I'll borrow my brother's car tomorrow. It's a lot more dependable than mine."

He flipped the ignition and started the engine. "If you need to use one of the ranch trucks, just let me know."

"Thank you."

As Jake pulled away from the Plymouth and proceeded down the long, graveled drive, he slid a glance at Diana. A black purse rested in her lap, and she fiddled with a safety pin that held the broken strap in place.

Helping women in distress wasn't his usual style. What did a guy like him have to offer anyone on the verge of tears? But for some reason, ever since Maggie moved in, ever since he started opening himself up to the kids, he'd softened. And frankly, it scared him.

He shot another glance at Diana and decided to change the subject, to find some solid ground. "How'd it go today? Did you find your way around the office?"

"I sure did." Her expression brightened, and for a moment, he took pride in the fact he'd been able to make her feel better, that he'd gotten her mind off her troubles. "It took a little while to get my bearings, but I've got things organized pretty well, and there's a bunch of checks ready for your signature."

"Great." Jake pulled onto the highway and headed toward town. "I'll sign them tonight, and you can mail them out tomorrow."

"I sure hope Rosa doesn't mind the way I organized things," Diana said. "I don't want to step on her toes."

Jake had intended the bookkeeping position to be temporary until Rosa returned. He always prefaced any comments related to commitment of any kind with words like "temporary" or "for the time being." It made pulling back much easier.

But Rosa had her hands full, running the house and chasing after kids, and he'd felt guilty about dumping the bookwork on her, too. Besides, Diana really needed the work, and he was in a position to help. "If you want the job, it's yours, Diana. But I hope you don't expect much help from me. I hate sitting behind a desk."

The petite brunette lowered her head, closed her eyes and whispered something.

He furrowed his brow. "What's the matter?"

She looked up and smiled. "I was just thanking God before I thanked you."

Jake hoped she wasn't going to get religious on him. He needed someone he could trust in the office, and she fit the bill. It was as simple as that. "No need to thank me."

"You don't know how badly I need to find a little house of my own, someplace where the girls and I can make a home for ourselves."

"Living with your old man is that bad, huh?"

"Let's just say that I want my daughters to have something different than the home life I had as a child. My dad is so fussy about keeping bedrooms clean and voices low." She blew out a weary sigh. "You have kids, Jake, so you probably know what I mean. Giggles, shrieks, messes and spills come with the territory."

Jake was still learning what kids were all about, but he figured childhood should be free of barbwire boundaries and criticism. His heart, what there was of it anyway, went out to the two little girls he hadn't met.

Again his thoughts had taken an out-of-character twist, not just tweaking a sympathetic vein, but causing him to actually consider ways to help. And again he credited Maggie and the kids for the change. They had sabotaged his defenses, making him wonder if he wasn't quite the loner he'd always thought himself to be.

He'd never been a family man, had never felt comfortable around kids. But then Maggie had suggested he spend more time with Kayla. He'd fought it at first, but when he could spend time with the girl on his own terms, it had worked out just fine.

Maybe that was the trick, doing things his own way. He cast another glance at his passenger. He wished he could do something other than provide Diana a job. Of course, he could offer her and the kids an occasional break, maybe even invite them out to the ranch.

Kayla would probably enjoy having some little girls to play with. And Maggie might like having a woman friend to talk to.

Shoot. Why not this weekend? He gripped the steering wheel tighter, as though reminding himself he was still in the driver's seat, still in control of how this all played out. "I'm taking Maggie and the kids to the swimming hole on Saturday. I thought we might have a picnic and let the kids get wet and muddy. Do you and the girls want to join us?"

Diana flashed him a bright-eyed smile. "Are you kidding? We'd love to."

He hadn't expected her enthusiastic response, but he was glad she appreciated the invitation. "Then it's set. I'll tell Maggie and the kids tonight."

"I'll bring my blue-ribbon potato salad. It's always been a big hit at church potlucks. And I make a killer chocolate cake." She paused, then glanced his way. "If it's all right with you. I guess I should have asked what you had planned in terms of food.''

Hell, his *plans* hadn't gotten that far. ''That sounds good to me.''

And, surprisingly, so did the idea of a picnic at the lake.

Jake still didn't see himself as a father and would never fall readily into the role. His old man hadn't been much of a role model, not after his mom died, but Jake supposed he'd learned what *not* to do. But he still felt as though he would fail miserably at what he *should* do.

A small flicker of hope sparked somewhere inside, deep in the dark and unused portion of his heart. Jake might not make a very good dad, but he was looking forward to taking the kids out to the old swimming hole on Saturday. To watch them splash in the water, maybe teach them to swim.

A slow smile tugged at his lips.

If Diana would watch the kids on the shore, maybe he could talk a certain, pretty doctor into climbing that oak tree and swinging across the lake.

He wanted to see Maggie loosen up again, hear the bubble of her laughter. See her eyes light up with youthful pleasure.

And he wanted to be the one who put that smile on her face.

Dinner had been especially quiet, and Maggie assumed that was because she and Jake couldn't very well discuss things in front of little ears. And maybe because they both needed time to sort through what had happened.

Memories of their lovemaking had followed her throughout the day, and as much as she preferred to put those passion-laden thoughts out of her mind until she and

Jake had a chance to talk, she'd continued to relive each touch, each kiss, each earth-shattering climax.

But how did Jake feel about the intimate turn their relationship had made? Did he want to take her to his bed again? Or had he decided they should maintain a platonic friendship?

"Uncle Jake," Kayla said. "Will you watch *Clancy's Magnificent Adventure* with us? It's a really good movie."

"I'd better help Maggie with the dishes," he said, lifting Sam from the high chair. "Maybe some other time."

"I don't need any help," Maggie said. "Besides, that movie is supposed to be very entertaining for adults and children."

Kayla clapped her hands. "Oh, goody! I'll go get the movie and turn on the DVD." Then she dashed out of the kitchen as quickly as her stilted gait would allow. Sam shrieked and followed after her, the little black-and-white pup on their heels.

"Ah, Maggie." Jake smooshed up his face, like a kid looking at a heaping plate of brussels sprouts. "It's that computerized cartoon, isn't it?"

"Yes, and believe it or not, it's received high ratings from both parents and children. I'm sure you'll enjoy it. And so will the kids."

His eyes beseeched her to let him off the hook. "Are you sure you don't need my help?"

"Positive," she said, giving him a competent smile instead of using his assistance as an excuse to speak to him alone. As much as she wanted to talk about what had happened last night, about what to expect tonight, standing over a sink of dirty dishes didn't seem to be the right place or time to discuss a relationship. "The kids have already had their baths. Why don't you help them put on their pajamas."

He grumbled, but left her in the kitchen.

Alone with her thoughts.

Dozens of questions swirled in her head, but none of them badgered her more than the dreaded but proverbial, Was it good for you?

It had been utterly fantastic for her. But then, Jake would know that. Wouldn't he? The man seemed to read her body like a love letter, to play it like a mystical harp. And Maggie hadn't kept her response to his touch a secret.

When she and Tom were married, she'd always been a quiet lover. But not last night. Several times she'd had to stifle a moan, a cry. And emotional words had tumbled around in her mouth, begging to break free. Words like "I love you," which she couldn't possibly mean.

Or could she?

Did her feelings for Jake go beyond desire? Given time and the opportunity to see how this relationship progressed, could she fall in love with Jake?

Maybe, she realized, but there was nothing for her in Texas if she intended to practice medicine. And Maggie wouldn't give up her career for anyone or anything. She'd fought too long and too hard to achieve her medical degree and a specialty in pediatrics.

The title of doctor was more than a part of who she was. It was her life, her identity. Her destiny.

No, she couldn't fall in love with Jake. Their relationship didn't stand a chance of blossoming into something of substance. And it bothered her that the zany idea had even crept into her consciousness.

Look what making love to Jake had done to her. It had her thinking all kinds of weird, irrational things.

But love had nothing to do with it.

Once they sat down and discussed what had transpired

last night, she could find some balance and rid herself of wild thoughts of romantic love and those sudden, unwelcome twinges of jealousy that seemed to spring up out of nowhere.

If she and Jake could just talk things over, she'd feel much better.

Maggie needed to know where she stood with him. Or, more important, where she *wanted* to stand with him.

She puttered around the kitchen, wiping down counters she'd already cleaned, then decided to take a peek in the family room and check on the children.

The sight on the sofa made her breath catch. And her heart swell.

The rough-and-tumble cowboy sat with his arm around Kayla and Sam nestled on his lap. The little boy sucked his thumb, while clutching his tattered yellow blanket. His sister held the sleeping pup.

Jake, his eyes transfixed to the animated scene on the big-screen television, brushed his lips across the top of Sam's head, as though savoring the scent of baby shampoo and the softness of downy fine hair.

Deciding to allow them time alone, time to bond, Maggie quietly stepped away from the doorway and went to her private bathroom, where she would draw a nice, hot bubble bath, a luxury that had become her custom in Texas.

Back home she'd been inclined to take showers, although she wasn't sure why. Time maybe? Too busy to pamper herself?

Maybe, but she suspected there was a psychological healing that took place while soaking in the bath. If that were the case, her mind, body and soul were on the mend.

She certainly hoped so. When she moved to California, she intended to throw herself into her work.

*   *   *

A knock sounded at the bedroom door as Maggie dried herself using a fluffy white towel.

"It's me," Jake said. "Can I come in?"

After the unbridled passion and multiple climaxes they'd experienced the night before, she should have thrown open the door without a care, met him wearing nothing but a playful smile and raging desire. But she couldn't bring herself to do something so blatantly direct. For some crazy reason, she felt shy. Nervous and apprehensive, like a virginal bride on her wedding night.

She quickly slipped on her robe, then opened the bedroom door and stood aside. "Sure, come on in."

Instead of entering, he stood in the doorway, his gaze slowly drinking her in and inflaming the nervous anticipation that swirled in her belly.

He reached up and stroked her cheek with the knuckles of his hand. "Will you join me out in the backyard?"

Go outside? Maggie had no idea how long she'd soaked in the tub. But surely, it was past the children's bedtime.

"What about Sam and Kayla?" She glanced at her wrist, only to realize she'd left her watch on the bathroom counter.

"Sam nodded off in my lap. I put him in his crib, then, after Kayla and I made a bed for Oreo in the barn, I sat on the foot of her bed for a few minutes and talked to her about a new saddle for Sunflower. I'm not into bedtime stories like you, Magpie, but it worked just the same."

Yes, she supposed it would. And it pleased her to see that Jake was beginning to accept the role of father. She had no doubt he'd make a good one.

"Now, it's our time." His eyes seemed to tug at the sash of her robe, to peel the soft chenille from her shoulders.

Unable to trust her voice not to betray either her jumpy nerves or her growing arousal, she nodded.

"It's a little cool out this evening, but not too bad. Why don't you slip into something warmer, while I get us something to drink. Would you like coffee? Wine?"

What she wanted was to pull him into her room and let him wreak magic on her body and soul, but she didn't have the guts to admit it.

"I'll have wine," she said, wanting something to take the edge off her nerves. "I'll just be a few minutes."

"Take your time," Jake said. "Although seeing you half-dressed is making me have second thoughts about taking you outside rather than to bed."

Warmed by his words, Maggie smiled. "Thank you. I think."

He kissed her brow, enveloping her in a woodsy scent of musk, then left her alone to dress.

She fought the urge to primp and, after slipping on a pair of jeans and a sweatshirt, took time only to run a brush through her hair. Excitement struggled with nervousness, but the time of reckoning had arrived. She and Jake needed to talk. And they both knew it.

As Maggie stepped onto the back porch, a nearly full moon loomed overhead. The scent of night-blooming jasmine filled the air, causing her to remain where she stood and enjoy the sights and sounds of an autumn Texas evening. Somewhere in the distance, a night owl made a haunting sound, calling, it seemed, to attract a mate.

She looked out into the darkened, grassy yard and spotted a flickering candle, an open bottle of wine and two glasses sitting on a small table that flanked the lawn swing. Jake sat under the canopy, swaying gently, watching her but not saying a word.

Touched by the romantic side of Jake she hadn't expected, Maggie stepped off the porch and walked toward him. She'd just as soon get this dreaded conversation over with, because this whole affair, or whatever it was, had set her nerves on end, as well as her senses.

And for a woman who thrived on control, she didn't like feeling unbalanced.

Jake stood. "Have a seat."

Maggie complied. She didn't know what he had in mind, but she let him take the lead. He poured a glass of wine for them both and handed her one. She thanked him.

He sat beside her, and the swing swayed with his added weight. "I'm starting to get the hang of this daddy stuff."

"I know." Maggie was glad to see him drawing close to the kids. He needed them as badly as they needed him. She took a sip of Chardonnay, then turned in her seat and faced him. "I never expected you to have a romantic side."

Romantic side? Him? No way, Jake thought. But the truth jarred him like a flat tire hitting a speed bump. He'd grown soft and sappy since Maggie had come. He glanced at the table and, shrugging off his efforts to make the evening special, nodded toward the candle and wine.

"You mean this stuff?" He had an urge to sit in the dark, rather than admit he had actually thought about something like ambiance. "Candles keep the bugs away. Besides, it's dark out here."

"Oh." Her voice sounded soft. Disappointed.

He wished he'd been brave enough to say that she deserved some special treatment. That he wanted to be alone with her, having nothing between them but the night wind to carry their words.

Great. Now he was a frigging poet.

This was one conversation that needed derailing. Fast.

Before he said something really stupid. And something he didn't mean.

"I'd like to take you and the kids out to the lake on Saturday. Maybe make a picnic lunch and invite Diana and her girls to join us. I thought Kayla might like to meet some girls her own age."

He'd expected Maggie to brighten at the suggestion since she'd been pushing him to spend more time with the kids, but she seemed to ponder the idea before responding. Then she broke into a gentle smile. "I'm sure the children will love that."

"Yeah." Jake dragged a hand through his hair, then dropped his arm to his side. "You know, I'm still afraid that I'm going to let them down someday."

"You probably will." She took his hand and gave it a gentle squeeze. "No one is perfect."

She had *that* right.

He pulled their clasped hands close, resting them on his thigh, then slid her a crooked grin. "But you're pretty damn close, Magpie."

"No, I'm not. Not really."

They sat for a while, enjoying the peaceful evening, then Maggie spoke. "Jake, we haven't talked about what happened last night."

Why did women always have to talk about something that was best left alone? "Is there any reason to?"

"Yes. How are you feeling about it?"

"Feeling?"

"You know," she said. "Are you sorry?"

"For making love to you? Hell no, I'm not sorry. It was good, Maggie. Damn good."

"I'm glad you thought so. I did, too, but we didn't get a chance to talk about it."

"What's talking got to do with it? Our bodies did the

talking last night. And I don't know about yours, but mine is aching to love you again.''

She nibbled on her bottom lip. It seemed like there was something weighing on her mind, but Jake had never been one for chitchat.

He drew their clasped hands to his mouth and kissed her knuckles. ''Want to make love under the stars?''

She burst forth with a nervous giggle, breaking the tension, it seemed. ''You've got to be kidding.''

''Not at all.''

''We can't do that,'' she said, as though trying to convince Sam and Kayla of the difference between right and wrong.

''Why not?''

She paused, and he figured she might be thinking the whole idea had a lot more merit than she wanted to admit. ''I don't know. Maybe because I'm too staid and proper to do something so wild and daring.''

''I guess I'll have to work on your staid and proper side.''

''Maybe so,'' she said.

He wondered whether he'd detected a wicked little glimmer in her eyes, a hint that she might be a hell of a lot more wild and daring than she suspected. ''Well, then, I suppose I'll have to settle for making love in a bed tonight.''

''I'd like that.'' Maggie looked up at him, her eyes laden with passion.

Jake took the nearly full wineglass from her hand and placed it, along with his, on the side table. Then he slipped his arms around her and pulled her close. ''I'm done talking, honey.''

He supposed she was done, too, because she leaned forward and placed her lips on his. As she opened her mouth, allowing his tongue to mate with hers, the kiss intensified. And so did the desire to take her right here in the backyard, in the moonlight.

His hands slipped under her sweatshirt, finding her breasts free of a bra. So soft, so full, so ready to be laved and caressed. As he thumbed her nipple, her breath caught.

The swing groaned and creaked with their movements. If the darn contraption had been bigger and longer, Jake might have suggested they stay outside, in spite of Maggie's reservations about making love under the stars.

As it was, he just wanted to love her, caress her, stoke the fire that raged in them both and bring on another star-bursting climax that engulfed them in waves of pleasure.

They moved to allow their hands to explore each other, to allow his arousal to press against her.

Without warning, the swing jerked to the right, and they both froze, afraid the darn thing would collapse under them. Their eyes caught, and they broke into laughter.

"This isn't working out very well," Maggie said.

"You're right." Jake kissed the tip of her nose. "Come with me."

He stood and reached for her hand, drawing her to her feet. "You bring the wineglasses, and I'll take the bottle and candle."

Jake meant to carry the implements of romance into the bedroom, but something told him he and Maggie wouldn't need any props.

Chapter Thirteen

From the moment Kayla learned of the upcoming picnic, the countdown began. And when Saturday finally arrived, the sun shined bright, its warmth tempered by a gentle breeze, much like the early days of summer rather than midautumn.

Stretched out beside Diana on the old, green-and-brown plaid blanket they'd placed on the shore, Maggie watched the children laugh and play with Oreo in the dappled shade of a sturdy oak.

Becky, Diana's oldest daughter, was a pretty girl, with long blond hair and a splatter of freckles across a turned-up nose. The tall ten-year-old took an instant liking to Sam and hovered around him like a mother hen—a job Kayla had always taken on in the past. Yet there was no jealousy.

Kayla had a brand-new friend with whom to play, a dark-haired child with blue eyes the color of her mother's.

After only a few shy moments when the girls were first introduced, Jessica and Kayla bonded quickly.

"It sure is nice to see the kids having fun," Diana said. "I'm glad they've hit it off so well."

So was Maggie. It was important for children to socialize. And she couldn't think of a better place to form bonds of friendship than here by the lake, where she and Jake first became friends.

Jake removed his hat and placed it on the side of the grassy knoll on which he sat. "I haven't seen Kayla this happy in a long time."

"Except when you take her riding on Sunflower," Maggie reminded him. The lessons had become a daily adventure Kayla looked forward to. And Maggie suspected Jake did, too. The expert horseman seemed to thrive on sharing his knowledge and skill with his niece.

Jake looked at Maggie and smiled. "Yeah. Kayla brightens up on those days, too."

They hadn't talked about their relationship since the evening on the back porch, but it no longer bothered Maggie that they didn't. There really wasn't anything more to say. They had a commitment to each other for the next month or so, then she would move on to California.

Still, Maggie feared the real reason she didn't press Jake to talk was because, deep inside, she didn't want to discuss what would become of their relationship when she left.

And their lovemaking needed no discussion. What had started as incredibly good had only gotten better. Still, Jake left the bed each morning while Maggie slept. And if she had any complaint at all, it was not waking in his arms.

"Hey, girls," Jake said, as he removed his boots and socks. "Anyone want to have a rock-skimming contest?"

"What's that?" Kayla asked.

"If you'll help me gather some small stones, I'll show you." Jake stood and peeled off his shirt, baring the broad, muscular chest Maggie loved to stroke and caress in the still of night.

He slipped off his jeans, revealing a pair of swim trunks underneath. Maggie couldn't help but stare, mesmerized by his movements, the perfection of his body in the glimmering sheen of the sun.

Whoa. She reprimanded herself for having a lover's feelings during a family outing and turned her attention to the children.

"Come on, Sammy," Becky said, taking the little boy by the hand. "Let's collect some stones."

Kayla held up a rock the size of a man's fist. "I found one, Uncle Jake."

"That's too big." Jake stooped and snatched a smaller one to show her. "We need to find more like this."

In no time at all, the children had gathered a pile. Then Jake showed the finesse it took to skim a stone across the water.

Not to be outdone, Sam took a rock and chucked it into the lake, squealing gleefully when the water splattered.

"Not like that," Becky said. "Try it this way."

Sam looked at the girl like she was crazy, then swung back his little arm and threw another stone into the water with a splash. Rock chucking, it seemed, was far more appealing to a little guy like Sam.

Maggie laughed. She enjoyed watching the little boy explore the world around him. She loved Sam. And Kayla, too. Never had two children touched her heart like these two had. She would miss them a great deal when she moved to California.

And she'd miss Jake, too. More than she cared to admit.

The realization struck her like a shot in the dark.

Her feelings for him had grown into something more than friendship. How much more, she couldn't be sure, but she feared that she stood on the precipice of something strong. Something special. Something suspiciously close to love.

People often confused lust with love, but what Maggie felt went beyond physical compatibility. Their friendship had always been special. Jake made her laugh, made her view life in a new perspective. And as she watched his relationship with the children grow, her sense of pride in him grew, too.

No, her feelings for Jake were more complex than lust and sexual attraction, but Maggie wouldn't allow herself to give it any more thought. Falling in love with Jake was not part of her plan. She had no intention of taking a broken heart to California.

Leaving her thoughts on the back burner where they belonged, she tried to focus on the world around her—the birds flitting in the treetops, the dappled sunlight on her legs, the children trying their best to mimic Jake's deft throws.

When the pile of stones had dwindled to none, Kayla tapped Jake's arm. "Can we go swimming, Uncle Jake? Please?"

"Sure. Did you bring your bathing suit?"

"I did!" Jessica lifted her pink shirt and showed him an orange-and-yellow polka-dot swimsuit. "See? It's underneath."

"Me, too," Kayla pulled up her red blouse, flashing a colorful mermaid on the front of her turquoise-blue swimsuit.

"Sammy," Becky said, squatting before the toddler.

"Do you have your trunks on?"

Maggie hadn't been able to find a swimsuit in his chest of drawers. "Honey, Sam will have to swim in his shorts. Let me take off his diaper, though."

Diana reached for a canvas tote she'd brought along. "I packed water toys and some floaties Sam can wear on his arms. And I've got more sunscreen, too. Maybe you should all have a second coat."

Moments later, Jake and the kids waded into the water while Maggie, who'd promised to baby-sit Oreo, held the puppy in her arms.

When Maggie glanced across the blanket at Diana, the pretty brunette smiled sweetly. "Thank you for including us."

"I'm glad you came," Maggie said, meaning every word. "The kids are having a ball."

Sam squealed with excitement, slapping the water with both hands, then blinking his eyes when the splash hit him in the face. Maggie and Diana laughed from their dry vantage point on the blanket.

While Jake taught Kayla and Jessica how to hold their breath and dunk their heads, Becky continued to play with Sam, teaching him how to kick his chubby little legs and propel himself in the water.

Whoever had invented those blowup floats for kids to wear had been a genius, Maggie decided. Sam was having the time of his small life.

"My girls haven't had this much fun since before their dad died. I'm so glad to see them laugh again."

"Well, this certainly will be a day for them to remember," Maggie said. "I'll bet they all sleep well tonight."

"You're right." Diana chuckled softly. "Jake sure has a way with kids. Who would have guessed that guy would have grown up to be such a good father to his sister's children?''

He had become a great dad, Maggie realized, and he'd developed those latent skills that had lain dormant and untapped for years. "I guess Jake has found his niche.''

"He certainly has." Diana slowly shook her head and sighed. "You know, Peter was too busy with his ministry to just kick back and be a father. He always thought he'd have more time with the girls after the church found a building in which to meet, after the congregation grew to a respectable size.''

Maggie realized her own life had been focused in the same fashion. Like Peter Lynch, she'd also thought in terms of *after*. *After* she graduated from med school. *After* she established a practice. *After* she paid off her student loans.

When was the last time she sat in the shade of an old oak tree, stretched out on the grass, wiggled her toes in the sunshine, held a sleeping puppy in her arms, watched children laugh and play? She couldn't remember ever having done that as an adult. And for the first time, she realized what she'd been missing in her life. Since coming to Texas, she'd found pleasure in the simple things— nights on the porch, picnics by the lake, making love by candlelight.

Thanks to Jake.

"Someday," Diana said, "when the time is right, I hope to find a man who will treat my children the way Jake treats Kayla and Sam.''

"I hope you do, too," Maggie said, wondering whether the man Diana found just might be Jake, once Maggie moved on and was out of the family picture.

The thought twisted her heart into a knot.

* * *

While standing in knee-deep water, Jessica whispered into Kayla's ear. "You sure are lucky to have a fun uncle like Mr. Meredith."

Jake didn't think the girl meant for him to overhear her praise, but it touched him all the same. He continued to help the older sister with her swimming strokes, showing her how to cup her hands to make her arm movements more effective.

"I know, Jessica," Kayla answered, her voice an exaggerated whisper. "Uncle Jake is the best uncle in the whole wide world."

Kayla's agreement sent Jake's self-confidence soaring. For a moment, he nearly believed he could be a good father to the kids.

"Mr. Meredith," Jessica asked. "Could we come over someday and watch Kayla ride her horse?" The brown-haired little girl smiled, showing off a gap where one of her front teeth used to be. "Becky and me love horses."

Jake tossed her a smile. "If your mom says it's okay, I can find two horses just as nice as Sunflower for you to ride."

"Really?" Her green eyes widened, and her jaw dropped, as though he'd offered her a shopping spree at the biggest toy store in Houston.

"Really," Jake said, pleased that something so easy for him to do had made the children that happy. He'd never liked taking the guests out on rides, never wanted to waste his time showing them how to play cowboy, but teaching three little girls how to ride a horse was different. Much different.

"Mommy," Jessica hollered to the shore. "Did you hear that? Mr. Meredith said he would let Becky and me go riding on horses with Kayla. Isn't that cool?"

"It sure is," Diana said. She mouthed a "thank you" to Jake, to which he merely nodded.

But when he caught Maggie's eye, saw her smiling proudly, his heart did a somersault. It pleased him to know he'd scored points with her, too. Over the past week, he'd let down his defenses, little by little, letting Maggie claim just a little bit of his hardened heart. Not that he would actually allow himself to do something so stupid as fall in love.

That would be crazy. All Jake needed was one more person to leave him emotionally high and dry.

Instead of focusing on Maggie, he turned his attention on the kids. He smiled at Diana's younger daughter. "Of course, there *is* one condition."

"What's that?" the child asked. "We'll do anything."

He chuckled. "You need to stop calling me Mr. Meredith. My name is Jake."

"That's easy!" Both girls waded through the water, wrapping their arms around him and giving him a hug. "Thanks, Jake!"

"Yeah, Uncle Jake," Kayla echoed. "Thanks for letting my new friends come over and ride horses with me."

His niece tossed him a dimpled grin that made him realize just how much she appreciated hiking, swimming, riding horseback and having friends. He marveled at the change in her, in how she laughed and played like a happy child, instead of wearing that sullen pout he'd grown accustomed to.

He had wanted to do something special with Buckaroo Ranch, something other than cater to the rich guests who frequented the place, but up until today, he hadn't been able to come up with anything in particular that he wanted to do. Interestingly enough, a morning in the sunshine with three little girls triggered a wild-ass idea.

What if the ranch catered to children instead of adults?

The thought had merit, but then it took a strange turn.

What if the ranch catered to kids like Kayla, kids who'd been handicapped in one way or another and gave them a chance to enjoy a sense of normalcy and adventure?

Sheesh. What was wrong with him? Talk about impossible dreams: Jake didn't know the first thing about creating a specialized ranch like that. There had to be a ton of regulations required and unimaginable hoops to jump through.

A guy like him didn't have what it took to pursue something of that magnitude. Hell, Jake hadn't even had the gumption to finish high school. Not when the cards had been stacked against him.

He quickly dismissed the idea as ludicrous. Only a fool would set himself up for failure.

And Jake was no fool.

He glanced at the shore, where Maggie rubbed sunblock on her legs. She sure looked pretty today, wearing shorts like she had as a young teen. His gaze traveled to the new rope that dangled from the branch of the oak tree.

Could he coax her to climb with him, to swing out over the water and drop into the lake, like two kids without a care in the world?

"Sam and I are getting tired of the water," Becky said. "Where are the towels?"

"Here they are." Diana reached into the canvas tote.

Maggie took a yellow towel she had packed and bundled Sam up like a little burrito.

"Hey, Diana," Jake said. "Do me a favor and watch Sammy. Maggie and I are going to show the kids a trick."

"Sure." Diana scooped the bundled boy in her arms and plopped him in her lap.

Maggie furrowed her brow and looked at him as though he'd fallen off the barn roof and bounced across the yard on his head. "What are you talking about?"

Jake took her by the hand. "We're going to swing on the rope and drop into the lake."

"What do you mean, *we?* Have you got someone hiding in your pocket?" she asked. "I'm not climbing that oak tree and trusting a fifteen-year-old rope to hold me."

"I replaced that rope yesterday with one guaranteed to be heavy-duty. You'll be safe with me."

Kayla clapped her hands. "Please, Maggie. I want to see you and Uncle Jake swing from the tree."

"I'm too old for that kind of thing," Maggie said.

"Yeah, and if you remember, I'm working on that proper, stuffy side of you." Jake shot her a crooked smile. "Come on, Magpie. You'll have plenty of time to be staid and boring when you go to California. This is your chance to be free and daring."

She seemed to contemplate his words, which surprised him. He figured he would have to do a lot more coaxing.

"Oh, all right," she said, getting to her feet and placing Oreo on the grass beside the blanket. "But if I get up in that tree and change my mind, you have to promise not to force me to do something I'm not comfortable doing."

"Scout's honor," Jake said, lifting three fingers.

"You weren't a Boy Scout," Maggie reminded him.

"That doesn't mean I'm not an honorable man."

Maggie lifted the T-shirt over her head, revealing a red bathing suit that had once belonged to Sharon. Jake's breath caught as he took in the sight. He'd never get tired of looking at Maggie, at appreciating each gentle curve.

Funny thing about that ugly, one-piece swimsuit. It had never looked that good on his sister.

Maggie dropped her shorts to the blanket on which she'd been sitting. "Don't forget your promise."

"To let you back out if you get scared?"

"That's right."

Jake took her hand and gave it a squeeze. "Trust me, honey. You'll be glad you did."

Maggie wasn't so sure about that, but a wild side she didn't know existed prodded her to go back in time, back to the days when Jake used to show her how to laugh and have fun.

As she followed his lead, she clung to his hand, matching him stride for stride as they hiked along the path that led to the tree. "I'm not sure why I'm letting you talk me into this."

"Sure you are," he said. "As much as you try to maintain that serious, bookworm exterior, there's an untapped, playful side of you."

Was there? If so, Jake was the only one who'd seen it. The only one who cared enough to bring it out in the open.

"You go first," Jake told her, as they reached the gnarly tree.

She looked at the old wooden steps someone had nailed in the tree trunk years ago. "Are these going to hold me?"

"They held me just fine yesterday."

She turned her head and, not realizing how closely he stood behind her, met him face-to-face. For a moment, she forgot her question and merely studied the flecks of teal in his eyes, felt his breath upon her cheek. She struggled with the overwhelming desire to take him in her arms and kiss him for all she was worth.

"You've been planning this?" she asked, her voice husky and laden with an arousal she didn't want to pursue in front of an audience.

"Yep. I've been wanting to bring you up here all week."

"Oh yeah?" A smile tickled her lips.

"Well, I've got other plans, too. But thought I'd slip this one past you first."

"What kind of other plans?" she asked.

The intensity in his eyes nearly took the wind from her lungs. "Making love to you out here one night—under the stars."

The suggestion sounded better than the last time he'd mentioned it, and she had to swallow hard, just to get her breathing back on track. "You think about stuff like that?"

He slid her one of his bad-boy grins. "All the time."

As much as Maggie wanted to pursue the conversation, to find out what kinds of things he was fantasizing, she turned and climbed up the tree.

When she reached the branch on which they used to stand, she looked down at the water below. "I don't know, Jake. This is a lot farther up than I remember."

"Come on, honey. It's not that high. I'll hold on to you, and when we get way over the water, we'll let go. But I'll hold your hand all the way, just like I did before."

He *had* held her hand, that long-ago summer day. And it had been exciting. Exhilarating.

Jake climbed beside her, reached for the rope and handed it to her.

Heart pounding, she looked at him, saw a promise in his eyes. "You won't forget to hold my hand?"

"Not for a moment." He brushed a kiss on her nose. "Let's go, Maggie. Trust me."

And she did.

The rope swung out over the water with Maggie and Jake both gripping tightly.

"Let go, honey. And take my hand."

Just like before, Maggie bit her lip, then released the rope as adrenaline raced through her body. Jake reached out his hand, and she grabbed hold. As they dropped in a free fall, Maggie's worries seemed to drift away. And as she hit the cool surface, with Jake at her side, the water opened up and swallowed them both.

A nearly overwhelming flood of warmth filled her heart. The precipice she'd teetered on was gone, and she realized, like it or not, she'd fallen in love with her best friend.

It was a bittersweet revelation, and one she couldn't do anything about.

"Atta girl," Jake said, when they surfaced. He kissed her, and she closed her eyes and enjoyed the brief embrace.

She tried to shove the love she felt for him deep inside her heart, but it didn't help. Her emotions bubbled too closely to the surface. The kiss was over before she knew it, and she opened her eyes.

He wore that James Dean smile that she'd grown to adore and arched a dark brow. "Want to do it again?"

She didn't dare let go and trust him again. "I think once is enough for today. Let's head for dry land."

They swam to shore and followed the path back to the others, both, it seemed, lost in their thoughts. Hers were nearly overwhelming.

"That was super, Maggie," Kayla exclaimed. "Uncle Jake, will you take me up there to swing?"

"Maybe next time, honey." Jake snagged one of the towels the kids had used. "I've got to lower the rope so it will be just your size."

"And will you take me up there, too?" Jessica asked, her blue eyes wide and hopeful.

"Of course." Jake ran a finger along her rosy, little cheek and smiled.

"Hey," Kayla said. "When are we gonna eat? I'm starving."

"Then let's have lunch." Diana withdrew a bowl of potato salad from the battered foam cooler she'd brought from home.

Maggie slipped on her T-shirt and shorts, then reached into the blue-and-white ice chest and removed the sandwiches she and Kayla had made earlier this morning. In no time at all, they had the food displayed on the blanket, along with paper cups and plates, napkins, plastic utensils, a bag of sliced apples and oranges, a bag of pretzels, a thermos full of lemonade and another of iced tea.

"What a blessing this day has been," Diana said. "God sure has a way of working everything out for the good, doesn't He?"

Did He?

Maggie wasn't so sure.

Falling in love with Jake had complicated her life in a way she hadn't expected.

Chapter Fourteen

The wild idea of turning Buckaroo Ranch into a place for handicapped kids grew to an impossible dream, one that dogged Jake throughout each day and kept him awake during the night, long after Maggie had fallen asleep in his arms.

His original game plan broadened, extending beyond a ranch experience for kids like Kayla. He wanted to offer vacations for entire families of handicapped children. Maybe let the parents utilize all the amenities the ranch offered, including the gym and spa.

Yet the sheer magnitude of the scheme made his head spin. For a guy who had never allowed himself to risk failure, Jake had sure come up with a whopper of a way to belly flop.

But the more he tried to tell himself an idea like that was so far-fetched it wasn't worth considering, the more it grew upon him, taking root. The darn scheme actually felt good, solid.

And right.

Just before lunchtime on Tuesday, Jake rode into the yard. One of the stable boys offered to cool down his horse, so he handed over the reins and thanked the young man.

After washing up in the service porch, before lunch was on the table, maybe he'd wander into the office and ask Diana a few questions about the night school her brother attended.

And then again, maybe he shouldn't reveal even a hint of the crazy scheme he'd concocted. The last time he'd come up with a goal, other than one that was part of rodeo competitions, someone had managed to jerk the rug out from under his feet and lay him low.

He hadn't bothered to waste his time again.

So why had he come up with this wild hair now? Shoot, he didn't even know where to start.

There had to be a slew of information on the Internet. If he even had a basic understanding of computers, he'd start poking around at night, after everyone else had gone to sleep.

The adult night school over in Janesville probably offered a computer course, but hell, Jake hadn't stepped foot in a classroom in nearly fifteen years. And he'd never regretted it. Not once.

He'd been a troublemaker in school, with a chip the size of the Grand Canyon on his shoulder, and he'd grown tired of fighting the inevitable. When he walked away from Janesville High at the beginning of his senior year, jumped in the old Ford pickup he used to drive and laid a patch of rubber at the asphalt entrance, he vowed never to step foot in a school again.

But what about one little old computer class?

That was different, wasn't it? Lots of retired folks took those night classes, along with other guys like him. Dropouts. Girls who'd gotten pregnant and couldn't finish school.

Maybe he ought to drive on over to Janesville, check things out. What would it hurt?

As he entered the kitchen, he found Maggie at the sink, washing a head of lettuce. She looked up at him and tossed him that pretty smile he'd grown so used to seeing, the one that told him she thought he could hang the moon. "Hey, you're early. Lunch isn't ready yet."

"That's okay." Jake stepped behind her, placed a hand on each side of her hips and nuzzled her neck. She wore a citrus scent today, fresh and crisp. One that made a guy hungry to taste her.

She giggled and turned, facing him and lifting her mouth to his.

But the brief brush of her lips wasn't what he had in mind, and he deepened the kiss, teasing the inside of her mouth with his tongue, pulling her hips against him. Kissing Maggie nearly turned him inside out.

Looking forward to sleeping with her at night made his days pass nice and easy. What would he do when it came time for her to leave?

Nothing. It was for the best.

Her best, anyway.

His, too, he supposed, because he had always liked the idea of quitting while he was ahead. He would let go before he had a chance to let her down or disappoint her, but for the next four weeks, he'd love her the only way he knew how. And making out in the kitchen during the middle of the day seemed like a great way to start.

As the kiss deepened to the point of heavy breathing

and groping, Maggie slowly pulled away. "As much as I'd like to let this scene play out, it's not a good idea."

She was right.

"Where are the kids?" he asked, hoping they were napping, but doubting he could be so lucky.

"They're both watching a video on television and could come in here looking for a snack or lunch any minute." She brushed her fingertips across his cheek, mothering him, it seemed, but it didn't bother him a bit. "You've got a smudge of dirt on your face."

That didn't surprise him. His boots had been loaded with mud. "I had to help Earl fix an irrigation leak."

"I'm surprised that man is still working. At his age, you'd think he'd rather retire and enjoy the good life."

"Earl thinks ranch-living *is* the good life." Jake couldn't imagine himself leading greenhorn city slickers on trail rides at the age of seventy-eight. "But I gotta tell you, Maggie. He's slowing down."

Earl Iverson had worked at Buckaroo Ranch for as long as Jake could remember. He doubted any thought of retirement ever crossed the old man's mind, although a good-size beer belly and a chronic cough indicated his health might not hold out much longer. Jake had suggested he see a doctor several times, only to have the man wave him off.

Jake reached for a glass from the cupboard. "I'm worried about Earl's physical condition."

"Maybe he needs a checkup," Maggie said.

"When I mentioned that, he told me ol' Doc Reynolds gave him a clean bill of health back in eighty-two."

Maggie lifted her brows. "He hasn't seen a doctor in more than twenty years?"

"Earl's always been a tough old bird. A horse kicked him in the head once, knocking him senseless and splitting his scalp wide-open. It bled like a son of a gun and swelled to the size of a double yolker. When he came to, Uncle Bob and I had him loaded in the back of my truck to haul to the hospital, since we figured we could get him there before an ambulance made it out here.'' Jake clicked his tongue. "The old coot cussed a wild streak and climbed out.''

"Maybe I should talk to him,'' Maggie said.

"I don't think it will help.'' Jake reached into the freezer and dropped a handful of ice cubes into his glass. "He's not too keen on physicians, even a pretty one like you.''

"I think I'll have a word with him anyway,'' Maggie said. She looked at the tumbler in his hand. "Would you like iced tea or lemonade? I've got both.''

"Water will do.''

"Jake, why don't you check on the kids? I'll have lunch on the table in no time at all.''

"Don't make lunch for me,'' he said. "I'm going to run into town for a while.''

"Can Oreo and I go, too?'' a little voice asked from the doorway.

Jake looked over his shoulder and saw Kayla, with the black-and-white puppy in her arms and a hopeful gleam in her eyes. "No, honey. Not this time.''

"Why not?'' the little girl asked.

Because he didn't want anyone to witness this crazy adventure. "Because I need some time alone.'' The excuse sounded dumb, even to him, but it was all he could come up with.

When he glanced at Maggie, she wore a pained expression, one he couldn't read. Shoot, he didn't want to upset her. Everything had been going along just fine. "I'll get lunch while I'm in town.''

Then, before either Maggie or Kayla could press him for more information, he slipped out of the house.

Jake drove into Janesville and parked his truck across the alley from the storefront building where several shops had been converted into classrooms for the night courses offered through the Janesville-Winchester Union School District.

There was plenty of parking available by the office door, but Jake still fought the old demons that barked at him for coming on a fool's errand in the first place. School hadn't been easy for a kid whose drunken father couldn't keep a job or stay in one place too long.

And even though he could justify why he hadn't ever liked school, why it was easier to disobey the rules set by the administration, it didn't change the fact that Jake wasn't sure he could do the required work. Or pass the tests.

At this stage of the game, he didn't have much time to study, even if he had the skills needed for academic success.

He walked along the sidewalk, peering into store windows. A drugstore. A Laundromat. A used bookstore.

Up ahead, an older man and woman sat at a folding table. The man heated a tube of glass over a blue-hot flame. The woman sat before a display of his handiwork. Still in no hurry to barge through the night-school door, Jake lingered near the delicate, glass figurines. He found several pieces of interest, but one in particular caught his eye. One that made him think of Maggie.

"It's the only one of its kind." The matronly woman scooted her chair closer to the table. "Pretty, isn't it?"

It was, he realized. He picked up the fragile glass skillfully shaped to look like a lacey valentine. He couldn't see any particular use in it, but the delicate figure reminded him of Maggie's healing heart, of the kindness she'd shown the kids. The kindness she'd shown him.

He wondered what Maggie would say if he gave it to her. It was probably a frivolous gesture to purchase it for her. In the past, he'd never given a woman a gift. Not like this.

Yep, Maggie had made him go soft. And against his prior principles, he gave in to the silly urge to see a smile light up her pretty face.

"How much?" he asked the mousy-haired woman.

"Forty-five dollars," she said. "It's the most expensive one on the table."

Jake handed her three twenties, which she placed in a wooden cigar box that held their money. After giving him change, she carefully wrapped the heart in bubble paper, then bundled it in tissue and handed it to him.

He slipped the bumpy package in his shirt pocket.

Women read into things sometimes. Maggie wouldn't think he was trying to tell her something, would she? But he quickly shrugged off the worry. A woman like Maggie might make a great wife and mother, but she was dead set on her career.

A career that would take her to California in a few short weeks.

For a brief moment, a sense of loss washed over him, but he kept his head afloat. Her leaving before things became permanent or etched in stone was a good thing. Yet, he sensed watching her drive away from Buckaroo Ranch might be a hell of a lot more difficult than he'd ever imagined.

He'd gotten used to having Maggie around, to hearing her laugh, having her in his bed. But it was best that she go. They both had to get on with their lives.

Jake made his way to the office door, then taking a deep breath, walked inside.

An attractive, silver-haired woman looked up from her desk. She rose and strode to the counter where he stood. "Hello. Can I help you?"

Probably not, Jake thought. "I'd like some information on night classes."

"Certainly." She reached for an application and a pen. "The fall semester began several weeks ago, but it shouldn't be hard for you to catch up."

Oh no? Jake nearly walked out, then and there. Playing catch-up wasn't his style. He'd had to do plenty of that each time his old man got a notion to move on. "I guess I could wait until next semester."

"Actually," she said, "we do our best to accommodate our adult students. I don't see any reason why you should wait. Our teachers present the day's lesson and assignment in the first half of the class, then provide extra work for those wanting to get ahead or further explanation to those needing more time."

Been there, done that, Jake wanted to say. Still, the desire to learn something about computers seemed to glue his boots to the floor.

She extended a hand. "My name is Betty Lou Johnston. I do whatever I can to help adults reach their goals."

Oh yeah? Could she help him? Not too damn likely. Still, she had a friendly smile, with spunky green eyes. And she wore the same rosewater scent that his grandmother used to wear.

He shook her hand. "Jake Meredith. And I'm not convinced that you can help me."

She grinned. "Let's just see about that."

An hour later, Jake headed home. For the first time in years, an educator had given him reason to believe in himself. It made him wonder what a little kid could achieve if one of his first teachers had given him hope, instead of a daily scolding.

Betty had shared the story of her own nephew, a young man from a troubled background who became a psychologist and now worked helping kids in low-income families with two or more strikes against them.

Maybe Jake wasn't stupid. Or irresponsible. Or undisciplined and lacking focus, descriptions a host of teachers had tossed at him in the past.

Not that he wasn't a hellion growing up. There was no other way to describe him, he supposed, but being tough had been his way of standing tall. Of fighting back.

Betty Lou Johnston was a hell of a saleswoman, because she sold Jake on himself. And she signed him up for not only a computer course, but a series of classes that would help him brush up on skills he'd never polished and new skills that would enable him to pass the G.E.D. by Christmas.

Or sooner, depending upon how easy he found the classes.

"The sky is the limit," Betty Lou had said.

Jake didn't know if he believed that or not. But *if* he managed to pass the G.E.D. and get some computer skills, he might feel more capable of tackling the regulations required to establish a specialized ranch.

Fear of failing hovered around him like a cloud of trail dust, but he fought it off. As long as he kept his efforts a secret, he would be the only one to know whether he failed or not.

On the drive back to the ranch, Jake realized that more hung in the balance than a dream. Any chance of a successful relationship with the kids—or even a long-distance one with Maggie—depended upon him believing in himself, in believing he could make something of the ranch and his life.

He needed to know that the people in his life who mattered, the people he loved, could depend upon him to follow through, to do things right.

A ranch for handicapped kids. Could a guy like him take on something of that magnitude?

Maybe, if he could prove to himself that he could succeed at night school. Everything hinged upon him making this work.

Could he pass the G.E.D. requirements? Or any of the classes he'd signed up for? He wasn't sure. But the biggest question of all faced him now.

Could he handle the embarrassment of failure?

Maybe, if Maggie never found out what he planned to do.

After the kids went to sleep, Maggie joined Jake in the living room. The television displayed a rerun of one of the crime dramas Jake liked to watch, but instead of looking at the screen, he stood at the window and peered into the dark of night.

Maggie slipped behind him and placed her arms around his middle, resting her hands upon the flat of his stomach. He covered her hands with his, as though holding her, keeping her close.

Or had she merely gotten to the point where she read into everything he did or said?

Ever since she'd realized that she loved him, the words struggled to surface and make themselves known. But she couldn't very well dump her feelings on him. Not unless he admitted that he loved her, too. They'd made a commitment to each other, but that didn't constitute any lasting strings.

Hadn't Jake told her he couldn't offer her forever?

And even if he could, Maggie wouldn't take him up on it.

She leaned her cheek against his back and relished the woodsy scent that mingled with musk. She'd promised to help him out for six weeks, two of which had passed. Their days were limited, as were their passion-filled nights.

"What are you looking at?" she asked, even though she doubted he was gazing at anything in particular.

She didn't dare ask what he was thinking about. Probably because she was afraid it had something to do with her. *Them.* And a relationship that had no chance to grow.

He turned, and his eyes searched hers.

Looking for some kind of answer? she wondered. Or looking for love?

Ah, gee. There she went again. What made her think she could burden their relationship with a sentiment like that? Saying goodbye would be difficult enough, but knowing he loved her, too, would hurt them both.

And there was no way around it. Maggie was leaving— in just under a month.

"I'm not looking at anything," he said.

That must mean he was thinking, but as usual, he held back, kept things to himself.

"I've got a great shoulder to lean on," she said.

He smiled. "You've got a great shoulder to nibble on, too."

She placed a hand on his chest, felt the steady beat of his heart, lost herself in the warmth of his steady gaze. "It's yours for the nibbling."

They stood there for a while, transfixed but undoubtedly thinking separate thoughts.

"Wait here," he said. "I've got something for you."

"For me?" She cocked her head to the side. "What is it?"

"You'll have to wait and see," he said, before leaving her by the window and walking out of the room.

Maggie had no idea where Jake went, but when he returned, he had a lump of tissue in his hand. It looked more like a wad of trash than a gift.

When he gave it to her, she held it carefully and studied the crude packaging before opening it. As she slowly removed the tissue that revealed plastic bubble wrap underneath, she paused and looked up. His gaze on her didn't waver, yet there was a sweet, anticipatory glimmer in his eyes.

She removed the plastic wrap, and when she saw the intricate details of the heart-shaped glass, emotion nearly choked her senseless. Jake had given her a heart.

Was it a symbol of his love for her? Or just the closest thing to his heart that he was willing to give? Either way, the gesture touched her beyond measure.

"When you go to California," he said. "I want you to know how much we appreciated having you here with us."

We? Or *you,* Jake? Maggie longed to ask, longed to hear him say that he loved her, too. That he would miss her. But she wouldn't cater to the insecure, needy side that plagued her here in Texas more than anywhere else.

"It's beautiful." She wiped a tear from her eyes, unable to keep the emotions he'd triggered a complete secret. "Thank you, Jake. I'll cherish it. Always."

He gave her a crooked little smile, the kind a little boy offered when he'd given away a picture he'd colored all by himself.

She kissed his cheek, felt the bristles lightly scratch her lips. Not only did she love Jake, but she found herself loving him more every day. She couldn't admit it, though, and she would have to be content not to ask for more than he was able to give. More than she wanted to take back to California.

She took his hand. "Let's go to bed, Jake. I want you to love me."

Maggie doubted he would know that her words hinted at the bittersweet truth.

Chapter Fifteen

As another dawn broke over the Texas hillside, Maggie woke in Jake's bed, only to find him gone. As usual, he'd slipped away before the sun streaked the eastern sky with shades of mauve.

She blew out a weary sigh and climbed from bed.

Their last days together were drawing near, and their lovemaking had become more intense than before. It seemed as though they were both trying desperately to hold on, to enjoy the few nights they had left.

Jake was an exquisite lover, more concerned about Maggie's pleasure than his own. Or so it seemed. Still, she couldn't shake an ominous feeling that something was wrong.

The nightgown she'd discarded on the floor last night was now draped neatly across the foot of the bed. As usual. In fact, all indications were the same—nothing in their relationship had changed.

But suspicion gnawed at her.

During the past two weeks, Jake had left the ranch in the late afternoon and not returned until after the kids had gone to sleep. Whenever she asked where he was going, he mentioned an errand he had to run and would tell her not to bother keeping dinner warm, that he would pick up a bite later. In town.

But three or four nights a week?

Maggie stood before the beveled mirror that graced Jake's dresser and kneaded her temples. He was pulling away from her. And she didn't know why, although it seemed reasonable that he might be trying to protect himself from getting too close, from caring too much. The clock in her head ticked louder every day, as the time for her departure drew near.

But it wasn't just in the late afternoons and evenings that Jake would disappear. Each day he'd take off in the morning, sometimes on horseback, but oftentimes in his truck.

She didn't see him much anymore, other than in bed at night. Had Jake found someone else? Someone to replace her after she'd gone? Was he keeping up pretenses because of his promise to her?

Worry plagued her as she slipped out of his room and went to shower before the kids woke up. So far, Sam and Kayla had no idea that Maggie and Jake were lovers. From all outward appearances, they were still just friends.

But were they more than that?

Doubt followed her into the shower and out. And when she stood before her dresser and reached into the underwear drawer for a pair of panties and a bra, she blew out a ragged breath.

Stop that, she scolded herself. *Let it go.* She'd come a long way since her teen years and even further since she'd left Boston. There was no way she intended to go back to square one.

She glanced at the top of her bureau and saw the delicate glass heart he'd given her. She picked it up, held it carefully in her hands, felt the cool, smooth surface of the figurine, the delicate texture of the glass-laced edge. Why had he given it to her?

Because he cared for her, that's why. And her suspicions were unwarranted. Jake had agreed to a one-on-one relationship with her until she left for California. She had no reason to believe he wasn't honorable, that he hadn't kept that promise.

She would make a concentrated effort to trust him, to believe in him, because that was the right thing to do. It was the only thing to do.

Besides, she couldn't very well sit him down and ask for an explanation, behave like a suspicious harpy. But that's what she felt like, at least on the inside. She wanted to grab him by the ear and ask him what was going on. Shake him until his teeth rattled. Jump up and down and scream her frustration.

Thoughts of Jake with another woman turned her heart inside out.

If he had succumbed to temptation, found someone else, her sense of loss and betrayal would be devastating—a gaping wound to her heart and soul. And much more damaging, she realized, than the hurt she'd suffered when her ex-husband had left her. Why would this man's betrayal hurt more than Tom's?

The answer settled on her shoulders, cloaking her in understanding. Jake had been more than a lover, he'd been her friend and confidante for years. He'd touched her heart in ways no one else had and, at times, he'd touched her very soul.

Losing his friendship would strike hard and deep.

But Maggie wasn't wounded. Not yet.

And she wasn't a needy woman. Jealousy and fits of temper didn't become her or the respected physician she'd become. Carefully placing the glass heart back on the dresser, she recovered her professional demeanor. Damn those childish insecurities. And damn her if she let them follow her throughout the day.

She quickly dressed, then left her room. The minute she stepped into the hall, the scent of bacon and coffee accosted her, and she followed it into the kitchen, where Jake stood over a sizzling skillet, watching the strips of meat brown and curl.

He glanced up as she entered. "'Morning. Did you sleep well?''

"Yes.'' She'd slept very well. She'd just woken up on the wrong side of the bed. The alone side. "How about you?''

"Great.'' He snatched a coffee mug from the counter-top and took a sip. "In fact, I've slept better over the last few weeks than I ever have.''

Reason prodded her heart. *See?* They did have something special. Her worries were pointless.

"I stopped by the post office last night,'' Jake said, nodding toward a stack of mail on the kitchen table. "I didn't sort through it until this morning. There's a letter for you.''

Maggie glanced at the top envelope. Sure enough, it was addressed to her and sent by someone at the Pacific Pediatric Medical Group. She'd called them before leaving Boston and gave them an address and telephone number where they could reach her.

"I wonder what they want?'' She tore open the envelope, withdrew the letter and began to read. If Jake was curious, he didn't give her any indication. Hoping he wanted her to share the contents, she gave him a brief rundown. "They're asking me to come earlier, if possible."

He didn't respond, yet she felt his concentration, his curiosity.

She read further. "Dr. Carlson, the man who is retiring and whose practice I'm taking over, has left earlier than expected. His wife suffered a minor stroke, and he took an early leave to spend more time with her."

Jake remained silent, lost in his thoughts, so it seemed.

Maggie didn't know what she expected him to say, but it would be nice to know he would miss her—like she would miss him. And in spite of her earlier worries, that loving each other would make her leaving more difficult, she wanted him to admit that he loved her. And perhaps suggest that she might find a comparable job in Houston or San Antonio and argue that a two-hour commute would be far better than a four-state flight.

"When will you be leaving?" he asked.

That wasn't what she wanted to hear. "I'm not sure. They really don't expect me to go until mid-November, which is the time I agreed to. They're just letting me know that it would be great if I arrived earlier than that."

"Like I said, when do you plan to go?"

"I'm not sure." She leaned against the counter and sighed. If Jake would just give her some idea of what he was thinking…and feeling… She waited for him to say something.

A knot formed in Jake's throat, blocking the words from escaping. As long as Maggie's departure had been in the future, he didn't have to think about her really going. About her leaving for good. But now it hit home.

And it struck hard.

His chest tightened, but he remained focused on the sizzling strips of bacon, on anything except her eyes. And the quick jab of her boot spur into his heart.

"I suppose I should try to get there earlier than expected," Maggie said. "But I hate to go before Rosa gets back. I don't want to leave you in a bind with the children."

He didn't see any reason why not. Over the years he'd gotten used to people leaving, like his alcoholic dad who committed suicide and left him with a critical uncle who didn't understand a kid's pain.

"Don't worry about us. Diana can help with the kids."

Her face paled, as though he was supposed to say something else. But hell, what could he say? *Don't go?*

He couldn't say that. And he wouldn't. Maggie's entire life revolved around her career and her achievements. Jake understood that. He would get over her; he didn't have any choice. But it would hurt like hell, and he doubted he'd ever be the same again. He sure wouldn't risk loving another woman.

Loving? Damn those sappy thoughts. Jake wasn't the kind of guy to risk loving anyone. Even the thought of love used to make him wince like he'd just touched an electric fence.

But the possibility of loving Maggie didn't scare him as bad as the thought of having her gone, of sleeping alone. Jake tensed his jaw. Sleeping alone had never bothered him before.

Before either of them could comment, a loud banging sounded at the back door, where Billy Ray Backus stood, hand raised, eyes wider than a skittish colt, mouth parted.

"What's the matter?" Jake asked.

"It's Earl. You better come quick. I think he's having a heart attack."

Jake cursed. "Where is he?"

"In the barn."

Jake and Maggie dashed outside. By the time they reached the stricken man, several ranch hands and a stable boy had gathered around.

"Give us some room," Maggie said, taking command.

As they stepped back, she dropped to her knees and quickly assessed Earl, his gray pallor, his vital signs. She glanced up at Jake, and he had a gut feeling that Billy Ray's diagnosis had been right on the money.

"How far is the hospital?" she asked. "Is there one closer than the one in Jackson Springs?"

"No." Jake answered.

"I ain't goin' to no hospital," Earl muttered. "Just let me die right here."

"And raise our workman's comp rates?" Jake asked, trying to best the man with his own crazy sense of logic. He felt for his cell phone, but he had left it in the kitchen. "Billy Ray, go call an ambulance."

"No," Maggie said. "Get your truck, Jake. We'll call on the road and have them meet us part way."

"But you ain't listening to me," Earl said, then grimaced.

"You're right," Maggie said. "You've just met a doctor who has more gumption than you."

"Billy Ray," Jake instructed, "go into the house and sit with the kids until Diana gets here. Her number is in the Rolodex on the desk in the office, so you might give her a call and see if she can come in earlier than eight-thirty."

"You got it, boss." Billy stood over his old friend. "You hang in there, Earl." Then the younger ranch hand did as he was told.

By the time Jake got his keys and cell phone, the men

had placed Earl into the truck. Maggie sat beside him, taking his pulse and talking softly.

Jake wasn't sure how much time had transpired, but he figured no more than it took to poach an egg. Still, it felt like forever, and the clock was ticking.

Nothing mattered but getting Earl to the hospital, getting him back on his feet. But Jake couldn't help thinking about the study time he'd planned to have.

There was a practice test for the G.E.D. tonight, and Mrs. Wofford, the instructor, had given him a review sheet to study. He'd meant to slip off to the lake this morning, as had been his habit when he wanted to read and concentrate in peace. But that game plan had been shot to hell.

In the scheme of things, the test lost its priority. He had to get Earl to the hospital and the medical care an E.R. could provide.

Besides, he told himself. How tough could the test be? All he needed was a C, then he knew he could pass the real thing.

"How's he doing?" Jake asked Maggie.

"Fine," she said. "Just fine."

But the intense frown she wore told him otherwise.

Thank God, and Dr. Maggie Templeton, Earl made it to the hospital. And according to the cardiologist on hand, the tough old buzzard might live.

Dr. Marshall stood beside Earl's bed in the Emergency Room and glanced at the chart in his hand. "We're going to have to admit you, Mr. Iverson."

"Like hell, you will," the tough-as-nails cowboy protested. "I got work to do. Just give me a pill or a shot in the ass, then hand me my britches."

"I'm afraid that's not wise, sir," the specialist said. "And the hospital and I strongly advise against it."

"For God's sake," the old man said. "I'm seventy-eight years old. I'd rather die than stay in here."

Maggie placed a hand Earl's arm. "You might not be lucky enough to have a massive coronary next time. Maybe it will be a smaller one, just large enough to leave you debilitated and unable to do much more than sit in a rocking chair on the front porch."

Her words seemed to have more of an impact than Dr. Marshall's, and Earl gave her a serious frown, before crossing his arms, blowing out a heavy sigh and grumbling a salty obscenity. "Oh, what the hell. Do what you gotta do, Doc. I don't want to live the rest of my life sitting on some park bench, fighting off a flock of pigeons trying to crap on me."

Jake stifled a smile. Maggie sure had a way with the old man. And seeing her in a hospital setting, watching her confer with the other physicians, nurses and lab techs who'd treated Earl made Jake realize what a damn fine doctor she was. She didn't belong on some dude ranch, washing dishes and changing diapers.

Hell, she didn't even belong in this small-town hospital. Maggie was meant for bigger and better things—things only a big-city hospital or clinic could provide. And even if she wanted to practice in Houston, the nearly two-hour daily commute would wear her down in no time at all.

And Jake wouldn't even suggest it, no matter how soft and mushy he'd gotten.

By the time Earl was settled into a room of his own, Jake and Maggie said their goodbyes, promising to come back and visit during the next few days.

Still, they didn't get back to the ranch until late in the afternoon. Time for Jake to head to school.

As Maggie prepared to exit the truck, Jake grabbed her arm. "I'm not going inside. Joe Fielder asked me to come by his ranch and take a look at a mare he just bought. His daughter wants to try her hand at barrel racing, and he thinks he's found the perfect horse."

Her face dropped.

"Will you be home for dinner?" she asked.

Maybe it was the stress of the day, the worry about Earl that had put that concerned look on her face. Or maybe it was something else. Either way, Jake had to go. He'd be late to class, if he didn't.

Finding excuses had been tough, but this was the first time he'd out and out lied to her about going someplace on the way to class. Not that Joe hadn't asked him to come by. That part was true, but there wasn't time now. Jake would have to reschedule on the way to school.

"No, Maggie, don't worry about me. Knowing Joe, he'll ask me to stay and eat with him. He's always trying to pick my brain and learn some of my training techniques." The dishonesty grated upon Jake, but he saw no way out. Not if he meant to keep his secret.

Of course, if he passed the test tonight, maybe he could tell Maggie what he'd been up to, what he planned to do.

She nodded, as though she understood, then opened the door and climbed out. She didn't say any more.

He thought about giving her a kiss goodbye, but when he glanced at the dashboard clock, he knew he'd be driving well over the speed limit in order to slide into his seat ten minutes after class started.

The test might be a practice, as far as Mrs. Wofford and the other adult students were concerned. But it meant a hell of a lot more to Jake.

If he passed this exam, he would know that he wasn't wasting his time with these classes. And if he didn't?

Then the idea of a ranch for handicapped kids and their families was out the window. And so was night school.

Mrs. Wofford called time, as Jake rushed to finish the final two pages of the test, but found himself unsure of the answers. Would she dock him for the questions he'd left blank? If she'd given any last-minute instructions prior to the test, he hadn't arrived in time to hear them.

He put his pencil down and raked a hand through his hair. Some of those questions were tough, and they'd taken much longer than he anticipated.

"I'll run the tests through the computer," the middle-aged instructor said. "If you'll give me a few minutes, I'll have your scores tallied in no time at all. Why don't you all work on the math paper that's due tomorrow?"

Then she strode from the small classroom, leaving Jake and the rest of the students to wonder how they'd done.

True to her word, Mrs. Wofford returned and passed out the graded scantrons. "As a group, you did pretty well on this practice run."

The woman's eyes met Jake's before placing his on the desktop. Her gaze seemed to apologize. And when he glanced at the score, his heart dropped to the floor like a rock tossed into an abandoned well.

Reality struck with a vengeance.

A pounding roared in his ears, and all the voices in the past hurled the same old accusations. *You don't ever listen. You don't focus. Buckle down and try, for goodness' sake. You'll never amount to anything.*

What made Jake think he could pass the stupid thing?

He wadded up the test and left the room, leaving Mrs. Wofford and the others staring at his back.

Later, he wasn't sure why he took time to stop by the office, why he bothered to tell Mrs. Johnston that he wouldn't be coming back. His instinct was to hightail it out of Janesville without looking in the rearview mirror. But for some reason, he felt as though he owed the woman an explanation, although he wasn't sure why.

Mrs. Johnston looked up from a file cabinet she was digging through. Recognizing him, she smiled.

He couldn't even attempt to smile back. "I'm taking off."

Her brow furrowed, and she closed the file drawer. "For tonight?"

"No. For good." He dropped the wadded scantron on the counter. "I'm not cut out for this kind of stuff."

The silver-haired woman glanced at the proof of his failure, then caught his eyes with hers, trying to connect, it seemed. Or figure out what he was thinking. He looked over his shoulder, double-checking that no one had come in behind him. That no one other than the kind, motherly woman could see him standing there, broken and down in the mouth.

"It was merely a practice test," she said.

Practice? Nope, it had been the real thing, an indicator of whether he could succeed, whether he was wasting his time or not.

She set the file she'd been clutching on her desk, then made her way to the counter where he stood. "I'm sure you'll do better next time."

"There won't be a next time."

Mrs. Johnston walked around the counter and wrapped her arms around him in a supportive, maternal embrace, offering sympathy he'd never had before. Sympathy he wasn't used to. But it didn't help.

Even the rosewater scent and its reminder of his grandmother did little to bolster his pride or raise his spirits.

Jake had failed the test. Not just this one, but his own.

And now he would return to Buckaroo Ranch with his dreams in a knotted gunnysack and his tail between his legs.

Thank God no one else would know his shame-filled secret.

Chapter Sixteen

Maggie paced the living room, waiting for Jake to get home. In the tiled entry, the handcrafted antique grandfather clock struck nine and marked the end of her patience.

Had Jake really gone to look at a mare, as he'd told her he had?

Maybe, but doubts tumbled in her mind. It would take everything she had to maintain a calm, professional manner and not meet him at the front door screaming like a fishmonger's wife.

She slowed her steps by the sofa and, placing her hands on the backrest, sighed. What was wrong with her? And more important, what was she going to do about it?

Confront Jake with her fears? Her insecurities?

No. She'd rather tell him it was time for her to leave. Time to revert back to the medical life she'd been trained to lead. And why not? Back in the real world of life and death, she took charge and relied on the skills she'd worked hard to learn and perfect. She was in control of her senses, instincts and thoughts. Like she had been today, at the hospital. While in the E.R., she hadn't experienced any of those weird feelings that plagued her here at the ranch. Not for a moment.

Boot steps sounded on the front porch, and as the door swung open, she turned and faced Jake, expecting a happy grin to mask his secrecy. Instead, she saw a grim expression. No lazy, carefree smile.

When she tried to read his serious demeanor, she spotted guilt. And shame.

Suspicion clawed at her throat, begging to be set free, but she fought if off with every bit of professional control she had left.

He placed his Stetson on the hat rack. "Kids in bed?"

"Yes." Her voice seemed to waffle, but not her decision to tell him she had decided to go to California early, maybe in a day or two. She couldn't take the insecurity or doubt any longer. She needed to escape to a world of reason and order.

He moved toward her, slowly. Deliberately. As though wanting her touch. Her forgiveness, maybe.

In spite of her reserve and the desire to question him, she stepped into his embrace and hoped to lose herself in his arms. And perhaps she would have easily fallen into place, next to his heart, had she not picked up a faint, unfamiliar fragrance.

The scent of roses.

Damn him. There *was* another woman. In spite of the desire to hold on to her temper, to fall back on her professional demeanor, all hell broke loose. The doctor in her disappeared, and the fishmonger's wife surfaced—a woman who'd just learned the man she'd thought of as her best friend, the man she loved, the man who had promised to honor their relationship had betrayed her.

She shoved her hands against his chest. ''Where in the hell have you been?''

His eyes studied her as though she'd gone stark raving mad. And she had. Crazy with pain, disappointment and anger. Crazy with a broken heart that might never mend.

She'd fallen in love with Jake—against her better judgment. His sister had said he was a ladies' man, but Maggie had hoped he could remain committed to her until she left town. Obviously, he hadn't cared enough about her to wait a few short weeks.

Her teeth had clenched to the point of aching, but she relaxed her jaw long enough to speak, to tell him words she had never uttered to her ex-husband. Maybe because she hadn't been as emotionally involved with Tom. Her feelings for Jake ran deep into her heart and soul.

''I thought you were a man of your word, Jake. A man of honor. But apparently, not. You couldn't even wait for me to leave before finding my replacement.''

Jake wanted to defend himself, to tell her he hadn't been with anyone else, to tell her he cared too much about her and their friendship to even look at another woman, but his sense of failure was too strong, too overwhelming.

What kind of defense could he offer? The truth? Hey, Maggie, I was out wasting my time, spitting in the wind.

Besides, other than laying his guts wide-open for her, what did he have to offer her? A life of scrubbing bathrooms, wiping noses and driving car pools?

Maggie was a talented doctor, for God's sake, with a top-notch practice waiting for her in California. She didn't belong on Buckaroo Ranch, and Jake was stuck here for good.

Their relationship had been doomed from the start. He knew it, and so did she.

"Aren't you going to say anything?" she asked, voice rising. "Aren't you going to offer me some kind of explanation for being gone nearly every night for the past two weeks?" She slapped her hand on the sofa back, although he figured she really wanted to smack him instead. "Damn it, Jake. You smell like some other woman's perfume."

Jake looked at her, at the pain-filled fire in her eyes. Maybe he should say something to appease her, but the only thing he had to offer was the truth. That he was a loser. That he'd let her down today; she just didn't know it.

Hell, he'd never been able to hold a relationship together, and he had no reason to believe this one was any different, particularly with her leaving. Besides, Jake could never give Maggie what she needed, even if he knew what that was. She had always managed to snatch her own dreams, fulfill her own needs.

Nope. This relationship was going nowhere. And the sooner they both faced it and got on with life the better. In a humane act, much like putting down an old crippled horse, Jake let her think the worst. "Does it even matter what I say, Maggie? You're leaving anyway."

Then, falling back on the best defense mechanism he had available, he turned and strode down the hall and into his room.

Maggie watched Jake walk out of her life, out of her heart. And when the bedroom door closed with a final thud, she crumpled to the floor, devastated by the blow and overcome with tears.

She had no idea how long she sat there, crying with gut-wrenching sobs, but she finally got to her feet and forced herself to move—one foot at a time. She walked into her bedroom and shut the door, but she couldn't shut out the pain of a broken heart.

Her eyes swept the room. Did she dare start packing tonight? Why not? Sleep would be a long time coming, if at all.

She turned to face the dresser and spotted the glass heart Jake had given her. At one time she'd thought it symbolized his love for her. She picked it up in her hand, and the hard, cold surface chilled her to the bone.

Without conscious thought, she threw the fragile figurine against the wall and watched it shatter into a hundred little pieces.

But the glass heart was still in better shape than her own.

Maggie didn't fall asleep until after midnight, but she still woke before dawn. By the time the kids climbed out of bed, she was packed and ready to go to California, yet she would wait until after Diana arrived to break the news.

She didn't have to wait long.

Diana strode through the back door and into the kitchen. "How's Earl?"

"I called the hospital last night," Maggie said, " and again this morning. He's cussing a blue streak, but holding his own. They hope to let him come home in a day or so."

"That's good to know. I've been praying for his recovery."

Maggie nodded. "Do you have time for a cup of coffee?"

"Sure." Diana slipped the shoulder strap of her purse over the back of the chair, while Maggie poured two cups and set them on the table where cream and sugar awaited.

"I'm leaving today," Maggie said, her gaze catching the surprise in Diana's eyes.

"It's a bit sooner than you thought, isn't it?"

Maggie wanted to share more, to say something to the woman who had become a friend. "Jake and I've had a...disagreement, I suppose you could say."

"Sounds like a pretty serious disagreement," Diana said, "if it made you want to leave early."

"He's been seeing someone else." Maggie blinked back tears that she'd thought had already been spent. "I know we didn't have anything permanent together, since I was going to California. But he couldn't even be faithful until it came time for me to leave."

Diana covered Maggie's hand with hers. "I take it that you became lovers."

Maggie braced herself for some sort of criticism. Diana had made no bones about her religious faith. Would she point out that a sexual relationship shouldn't be taken lightly? That it was Maggie's own fault?

"I love Jake," she said in her own defense. "And even though there was no future for us as a couple, married or otherwise, I made a decision and will live with the consequences."

Diana's smile reached deep inside Maggie, flooding her with understanding, rather than reproach. "Falling in love isn't easy, is it?"

"No," Maggie said.

"I'll pray that your heart heals and that, when the time is right, a special man will come into your life, one that loves you and is worthy of your love."

Would Maggie ever find a man again? A man who was honest and trustworthy? A man whose word was a promise? She was beginning to wonder if there was such a thing.

And even if there were, she couldn't imagine being in another man's arms. The thought was more than a bit unsettling.

Before she could respond, Kayla and Sam wandered into the kitchen.

"Sam wants breakfast," the little girl said. She glanced at the suitcase by the door. "What's that?"

"It's my bag," Maggie said. "I'm leaving for California this morning."

"Today?" Kayla asked, her eyes wide with disbelief.

"Yes. Diana will keep an eye on you until your uncle gets home." Maggie picked up her coffee mug and carried it to the sink. "I would have left sooner, but I wanted to say goodbye to you and Sam."

"But I don't understand," Kayla said. "Why do you have to go today?"

"I'm needed at my new job." Maggie glanced at Diana, hoping for some adult reinforcement.

"Yes," Diana said. "But don't worry, Kayla. I'll watch over you and Sam until Rosa comes back."

"I know," Kayla said. "But I don't want Maggie to leave us."

Maggie knelt before the child, her own heart heavy with grief and disappointment. "I'll give you my telephone number and my address. You can call or write whenever you want. And I'll call and write to you, too."

She hoped her words would help the little girl she'd grown to love, even though she knew a letter or a long-distance conversation wouldn't be the same. To her, or to Kayla.

The girl swiped a tear from her eyes. "Does Uncle Jake know you're leaving?"

Probably, Maggie thought. But he'd apparently left well before she woke up and hadn't come back. As far as she was concerned, their goodbyes were said last night. "We discussed it briefly after you and Sam went to bed."

"But he'll want to say goodbye. Can't you wait until later, after he gets home?" The little girl had such hope in her eyes that Maggie hated to burst her bubble.

"I'll have to say goodbye in a call or letter," Maggie said, although she would do neither. Whatever friendship she and Jake had shared, prior to his betrayal, was damaged beyond repair.

It was her own fault, though, and she had no one to blame but herself. Maggie had fallen in love with a charmer, a man who couldn't be trusted. She should have known better.

"Give me a hug." Maggie opened her arms. Tears clogged her throat, and she struggled to keep them a secret.

Kayla fell into her embrace and squeezed her tight. "You're the best baby-sitter in the whole world, Maggie. Me and Sam are gonna miss you a whole lot. Probably forever."

"I'm going to miss you, too." This time, the tears she'd been fighting won the battle. She sniffled, then released the little girl. "I need to give Sam a hug, too."

She scooped the little boy into her arms, savoring his baby-powder scent, and kissed his cheek. "I'm going to miss you, Sammy."

"Mag!" The small boy wrapped his chubby arms around her neck and placed a slobbery kiss on her cheek, leaving a wet spot she hoped would never dry.

Walking away from the kids was killing what little part of her heart Jake hadn't destroyed, but she had to go. She had to break away before Jake got home, before she had to face him again.

She grabbed her bag and purse. "Take good care of them, Diana."

"I will." The woman she'd once thought of as a rival embraced her. "I'll keep you in my prayers."

"Thanks," Maggie said.

But she doubted any prayers would help.

Maggie had been gone for three weeks and four days. Jake knew exactly how long she'd been gone, because he couldn't help counting the mornings he woke and found himself in a cold, empty bed.

The kids, too, struggled with her loss, even though Rosa had returned to work last week. Happy to see their much-loved nanny, they still missed Maggie. Jake wondered if his old friend had any idea how much the kids loved her. He sure did.

Kayla blamed him for letting Maggie go, for not talking her into staying, for not making her feel like part of the family.

Sam missed her, too, Jake suspected, because the little boy sucked his thumb more often and dragged his worn, yellow blanket everywhere he went.

Jake stood in the kitchen, a mug of lukewarm coffee in his hands, and listened to the muted sounds of children playing in the backyard where Rosa supervised them. Diana's two girls didn't have school today, since the teachers and school staff had an in-service day, whatever the heck that meant. Rather than have Diana miss work, he had suggested she bring her daughters to the ranch. He knew Jessica and Becky wouldn't be a burden to Rosa. The girls entertained both Sam and Kayla.

As the children's voices grew louder and footsteps sounded at the back door, Jake set his coffee mug in the sink and turned to face the giggles and chatter.

"Uncle Jake!" Kayla's smile surprised him, since she hadn't been happy since Maggie left. "Guess what?"

"What?" he asked.

"I kicked the ball through the goal three times. Yesterday I couldn't do it at all, but Becky kept showing me how and I tried and tried until I got it right."

"Atta girl," Jake said, pleased that she hadn't given up. The kid had met plenty of challenges head-on.

Unlike himself, he realized.

"And you know what else?" she asked, eyes glimmering with pride.

"What's that?"

"I'm going to play soccer when I turn six. Rosa said it's okay and that she'll take me to all the practices."

Rosa smiled at him. "If it's all right with you, of course. Kayla was just so excited. And I'm sure the experience will be good for her."

His first inclination was to say no. To worry about a kid with cerebral palsy running and competing with kids who didn't have physical handicaps.

"The soccer league was opened for kids of all levels and abilities. And the coaches seem to be kind and understanding. They teach good sportsmanship above all else." Rosa's gaze speared his, telling him she knew what he was thinking.

When he broke eye contact with Rosa and saw the Maggie-like determination in Kayla's eyes, he didn't have the heart to disappoint her. "Okay. If that's what you really want to do."

Kayla wrapped her arms around his thigh and squeezed tight. "It sure is, Uncle Jake. And I know that I won't be the best player on the team, but I don't care. I just want to do my very best. And I won't quit, no matter what."

Her words jarred him, momentarily taking him aback.

He'd never considered himself a quitter before. He just avoided anything that required beating his head against the wall. And there'd been plenty of walls when he'd been growing up. Still, Jake refused to give it any further thought.

He patted his niece on the back. "You've got the right attitude. I'm proud of you, Kayla."

He just wished he felt the same way about himself.

Chapter Seventeen

Jake tossed in bed, caught in the throes of a nightmare he hadn't had in years.

"*Come here, boy,*" his drunken, teary-eyed father said, words slurring, feet shuffling. "*I wanna talk to you.*"

The stench of cigarette smoke and stale alcohol hovered around him, and he couldn't bear to sit up another night. He had a test tomorrow, one that determined whether he'd pass the sixth grade and go on to junior high. His grades had been dropping, and he'd spent more than his share of time in detention. For once in his life, he wanted to do well, leave the elementary troubles behind and start fresh at a new school, with new teachers.

His old man sat on the mattress, causing the springs to creak and bounce. "*Talk to me, son.*"

Jake rolled over in the narrow, twin bed and put the floppy, sweat-scented pillow over his head. "*I don't want to talk, Dad. I'm tired.*"

His dad jerked the pillow away. "I'm hurtin', son."

"Go pour yourself another drink, Dad." Jake said as he pulled the blankets over his head and tried to get some sleep.

A haunting blast of gunfire tore Jake from his dreams. He sat up in bed, sweat beaded upon his brow. His heart pounded just as hard as it had that night, the night he found his father slumped over the dining room table, an empty bottle of whiskey to his left, a .38 Smith & Wesson in his hand.

Jake closed his eyes, but still relived the ugly reality. The blood he didn't want his sister to see. The nausea. The grief.

All the guilt he'd harbored for years rushed to the forefront, pounding him with accusations. Why hadn't he just listened to the old man sob?

Jake sat up and looked at the empty side of his bed. The side that had once been Maggie's. He wished she were here and able to chase away the demons with her gentle hand, her sweet caress, her wise words.

She would have held him close, told him it wasn't his fault. Reminded him that he'd been a twelve-year-old kid. And she'd point out who was really to blame.

His dad didn't need anyone's permission to have another drink. He was a grown man with two kids depending upon him. And he'd used alcohol as a means to escape his problems.

It wasn't Jake's fault, damn it. Bobby Joe Meredith hadn't cared enough about his son and daughter to face his demons, rather than drown himself with a bottle of ninety-proof.

Jake's dad had run away, leaving Jake to call the police. To close doors and block the bloody remnants of his dad's goodbye from his sister.

His old man had run away.

Jake buried his head in his hands, realizing he'd been running for years. From intimacy. From commitment, from a challenge.

He glanced at the clock. Ten o'clock—hours before dawn.

Mrs. Johnston would still be in the night-school office, since she worked from two in the afternoon until eleven at night. Did he dare drive out to Janesville now? He felt a desperate urge to fix things, an urge that wouldn't wait until morning.

After knocking on Rosa's bedroom door and letting her know he'd be gone for a while, he jumped in the truck and started up the engine. Few cars drove along the country roads and highways, which enabled him to reach the night school in fifteen minutes.

When he entered the office, the silver-haired woman looked up from her desk. She smiled as though seeing him arrive at this time of night didn't surprise her at all. "Hello, Jake."

"I'd like to return to class, if it's not too late."

Her smile broadened, revealing dimpled cheeks and a glimmer in her eyes. "I'm of the mindset that it's never too late."

Thank God for that. Jake needed someone to remind him that he still had time to make things right. He had dreams on the backburner that demanded his efforts. He lifted his hat and ran a hand through his hair. "I made a big mistake by quitting."

"Well, let's see if we can work together to rectify that."

Jake wished he could rectify his problems with Maggie, too. But he figured that was out of Betty Lou Johnston's league. Still those sappy urges came to the forefront, as they always did when he thought about Maggie, about how he loved her.

He loved her.

The reality of it jolted him to the bone. He loved Maggie. And he'd let her go away thinking he was a liar and a cheat. A man who wouldn't know how to treat her, if he had the chance.

Jake didn't have the chance to renew a lover's relationship, of course, but he could certainly work on patching up the friendship he'd ruined.

"Mrs. Johnston," he said. "Can I ask you a question?"

"Certainly." She looked at him with those maternal, green eyes. Springtime eyes, filled with hope and renewal.

Ah, sheesh. More mush and sappy stuff.

But you know what? he asked himself. He kind of liked that sappy, mushy side of himself.

"School isn't the only thing I ran out on. I ran out on Maggie, too. I let her think I didn't love her." He blew out a slow breath, releasing his secrets one by one. "Starting over in school is one thing, Mrs. Johnston, but how in the world do I ever make up for letting Maggie go without admitting how I feel about her?"

"What were you afraid of?" she asked.

"Of failing at a relationship. Of letting her down." Jake leaned against the counter. "And I've lost the best friend I'd ever had."

"It takes a brave man to admit when he's wrong, let alone face his mistakes like you're doing."

Did facing up to his shortcomings mean telling Maggie the truth? Apologizing and leaving the fate of their friendship to her ability to forgive? Jake nodded slowly, as everything began to fall into place.

As he turned to go, Mrs. Johnston called to his back. "Can I expect to see you in class tomorrow night?"

Jake paused in the doorway. ''I'm afraid not. Maybe next week. I've got to make a trip to California.''

He needed to tell Maggie the truth. He loved her, even if they could never be lovers again. Her friendship meant too much to him, and he didn't want to lose her.

It might be cheaper and easier to make a phone call, but what he had to tell Maggie was best said in person.

The next morning, Jake packed an overnight bag and left the children in Rosa's care. He caught a Los Angeles-bound flight out of George Bush Intercontinental Airport. He wasn't entirely sure where to find the Pacific Pediatric Medical Group, but he had a cell phone in hand and plenty of cab fare in his pocket.

As it was, the cabby, a tall lean fellow who had photos of his kids taped to his overhead visor, knew exactly where the clinic was. ''They're the top pediatricians in the county, if not the whole state,'' the man said proudly. ''Me and my wife wouldn't take our kids anywhere else.''

Jake didn't doubt it. Maggie deserved to work with renowned colleagues and at a first-rate clinic.

The cabby stopped in front of a white, Spanish-tiled office building close enough to the Pacific Ocean to attract seagulls over head. Jake climbed from the back seat and paid the driver.

''Check out the doctors,'' the cabby advised. ''You won't be disappointed.''

''I'll do that.'' Jake took his black duffel bag and walked up the steps to the front door of the medical group where Maggie had found her rightful place.

When he entered the vast waiting room, he found every chair filled and kids of all shapes and sizes everywhere. Some read books quietly on child-size beanbags clustered in a corner. A few older kids and the adults with them sat in a private area called the Teen Scene. He made his way to the front desk.

"Is Maggie… I mean Dr. Templeton available?"

The receptionist, a young woman with short, curly hair the color of Little Orphan Annie's, glanced up from her work. "Is she expecting you?"

"No." Jake couldn't help but wonder if the color was real or from a bottle. He'd never seen anyone with hair that bright of orange.

The woman's jaws worked on a wad of chewing gum. "I'm afraid she's behind schedule, like all of the doctors today. We've had three emergencies this morning, and now we've got appointments backed up."

When a young mother carried in a little boy with red eyes and a runny nose, she was quickly directed to a secluded waiting area for sick children, which Jake thought was an especially good idea.

"Now, let's see," the harried receptionist said, looking at Jake. "Oh, yes. Like I was saying, Dr. Templeton is very busy right now."

No doubt, Jake thought. For a moment, he contemplated leaving and finding a hotel, but he glanced at his watch. What the heck, maybe he'd just wait until the last kid had been examined. "Okay for me to sit here until she finishes for the day?"

"Sure," the young woman said, popping her gum. "Why not?"

When a nurse holding a file in her arms opened the door and called, "Katie Gove," a mother took her daughter by the hand, freeing two chairs.

Jake took one and settled in for a long wait.

At the end of a grueling day, Maggie headed for the front office, more than ready for an evening curled up in an easy chair, a good book in hand. Three broken bones, two hospital admissions and a laceration needing stitches had set her schedule off track for the entire afternoon.

"Is that it, Mary?" she asked the redheaded receptionist.

Mary, who'd recently given up smoking, chomped on the gum she used as an oral replacement. "Yeah. Except for the guy waiting to talk to you."

Maggie didn't feel like talking to another pharmaceutical salesman, not today. She just wanted to go home, put on a pair of sweats and soak her feet. She wondered whether she could put him off until tomorrow. "Which company does he represent?"

"I'm not sure, but he looks like a real, rootin' tootin' cowboy, if you ask me."

Maggie's heart dropped into her stomach. The only cowboy she knew was Jake. But surely it wasn't him. "Did he give you a name?"

"Ah, gee, Doc, if he did, I wouldn't remember. This day has been absolutely wild."

She was right about that. Maggie took a deep breath and walked to the hall that led to the waiting room. She turned the knob and opened the door.

When Jake looked up from a magazine, she froze.

"Hi, Magpie." He stood and sauntered toward her, taking her breath away, as well as a substantial bit of the anger he'd once stirred.

She didn't trust herself to speak.

"I have a confession to make," he said in that soft, Southern twang she'd missed.

Jake came all the way to California to admit that he'd cheated on her? It was a wasted trip, as far as she was concerned. Surely, he didn't intend to give her details.

He stepped closer, close enough for her to catch that

musky, woodland scent. Close enough to touch, but he kept his hands at his sides. "I love you, Maggie."

Her pulse began to race, and her knees threatened to give out. It wouldn't take more than a light breeze to blow her over. At one time, she would have done anything to hear him say those words. To know he meant them.

Why now? Why when it was too late to make a difference?

"There never was another woman, Maggie. But I did have a secret I was keeping from you."

No other woman? She wasn't sure whether she should believe him. Still, the words wouldn't come, and she stood before him, feeling like a cross between the village idiot and a besotted fool. She gripped the seat back of the nearest waiting room chair.

"I was attending night school."

She didn't know what kind of revelation she expected, but certainly not that. "Why in the world would you keep something like that a secret?"

"Because I made up my mind a long time ago not to set myself up for failure. And as far as I was concerned, I didn't stand a snowball's chance in hell of getting a diploma or a G.E.D."

"But why did you keep that from me? I would have understood."

"It made a heck of a lot of sense to me at the time." He jammed his hands in the front pockets of his jeans. "I figured I could handle failing, as long as no one knew what I was up to. It was a test of sorts, to see if I could finish something. And if I succeeded, then maybe I could be a better dad to the kids. Be a better man for the woman I love."

Maggie didn't understand his reasoning, yet she sensed

his sincerity. "You let me think you were cheating on me rather than tell me the truth?"

"That last night you were in Texas, after Earl went to the hospital, I had to take a practice test. But it was more than a practice test to me, Maggie. It was a chance to see if I could put some real plans into motion." He looked at her with battle-fatigued eyes. "I bombed the test that night. And I felt more like a failure than I ever had before. Maybe it was stupid, but I figured you were better off without me and the sooner you left, the happier you'd be."

She wanted to reach out to him, to take his hand, clutch his arm, but she tightened her grip on the seat's back instead. "And what do you think now?"

"That I should have trusted you with the truth. And that I should have told you that I love you before letting you leave. No woman will ever come close to replacing you in my heart." His eyes glimmered, and he tossed her that bad-boy grin. "Or replace you in my bed."

Maggie's cheeks flushed, and a warmth settled in her belly. Jake loved her.

Bubblegum popped behind her, and she turned to see Mary, the receptionist, watching and listening intently. Not about to become fodder for the office gossips, Maggie took Jake's hand. "Come on. Let's talk about this in private."

Twenty minutes later, Maggie let Jake into the front door of the small, ground-level condominium she had rented.

Jake removed his hat and scanned the sparse furnishings. "Nice place you have here."

Nice and lonely, Maggie wanted to say. Instead, she thanked him. "Would you like something to drink? I need to go grocery shopping, but I do have some apple juice, mineral water or wine.''

''After the day you've had, Maggie, maybe we should both have wine.''

Her day had been unusually tough, but the evening promised to be surreal and awkward, at best. She kicked off her shoes and padded into the kitchen. ''Then wine it is.''

When she returned to the living room with two glasses of chilled sauvignon blanc, she found Jake standing at the sliding glass door, looking into the garden area of the quiet condominium complex.

When he heard her enter, he turned and took the wine she offered. ''I've got something else to tell you.''

''What's that?'' she asked, completely surprised by his visit, his admission. His secret.

''I've got a real game plan, Maggie. One much bigger than night school.'' He'd always scoffed at her when she'd asked him if he ever had dreams or goals. This was the first he'd been willing to share. ''I'm going to make Buckaroo Ranch a place for handicapped kids like Kayla to attend, a place where they can feel good about themselves.''

The scope of his goal stunned her, but it also filled her with pride. ''If there's anything I can do to help, I'd be glad to.''

''Thanks,'' he said. ''I still have a lot of research to do. But I'm finding a ton of stuff on the Internet. I'm checking into insurance and government regulations. It won't be easy, but I'm determined, like you've always been, Maggie.''

She could see that. Hope had brightened his eyes, and his gaze snared hers, pulling her into his dream.

''You know,'' she said, ''I do foresee one problem.''

Jake tensed, and she thought he might be bracing himself for opposition. "What problem do you see?"

"You'll need more than a first aid course and a nurse's office. Not that you should expect medical emergencies, but with the major hospital so far away, you'll need to have a qualified medical staff available, just in case."

"You're thinking about Earl and the trouble we had getting him to the hospital." Jake took a swallow of wine, then glanced out the window as if he might find a solution.

"The children who come to your ranch will all have health issues. And the fact is, no matter how great your plan, you need to provide onsite medical care, if necessary." She placed her wineglass on the coffee table and crossed her arms.

He turned and slid her a crooked grin. "I don't suppose there would be any chance you would like to be the pediatrician on staff?"

Maggie swallowed hard. She hadn't been thinking of taking the job herself, although the idea sent her mind soaring. If Jake loved her, and she loved him, too, a long-distance relationship wasn't going to work. "The job offer has merit. I guess I'd have to think about it."

"How long do you need?" he asked taking another drink of wine and watching her intently over the rim.

"Well, it depends."

"On what?"

"Does that job offer include a marriage proposal?"

Jake sought her gaze, as though trying to gauge her sincerity. "Are you willing to marry me, Maggie?"

"I love you, Jake. And marriage seems like a solid game plan. Will you let me balance my career with being a wife and mother?"

"In a heartbeat." He set his glass on the lamp table and took her into his arms, drawing her close. She relished the scent of his cologne, the intoxicating feel of his body pressed against hers.

He drew her into a powerful kiss, one that spoke of promises and forever. When they came up for air, she smiled. "Marriage is going to place a lot of demands on you, Jake Meredith."

"What kind of demands." He didn't loosen his hold, didn't appear to be worried.

"I want it all."

He furrowed his brow. "What do you mean by *all?*"

"I want you to share everything with me, your heart, your hopes, your fears. No more secrets."

Jake cupped her cheek. "I'll give it my best shot, honey, but I've been a loner for a long time. Some habits are hard to break."

She placed a hand upon his chest, felt the warm, steady beat of his heart. "And there's one more thing."

"Lay it on the line, honey."

"No more leaving the bed before I wake up. I want to spend the rest of my nights holding you until the sun comes up.

He kissed the tip of her nose. "That one's easy, Magpie. I thought you liked getting a few extra minutes of sleep."

"I don't especially crave sleep when I'm in bed with you." Then she took him by the hand and led him into her bedroom, where they would celebrate the love they felt, the promises they made.

Taking their time, they undressed each other, savoring each glimpse, each touch of skin and heat. As Maggie stood before Jake, bare and free of the old insecurities at last, she kissed him with all her heart and soul, and he returned her love, stroke for stroke, word for word.

Two friends had become lovers and partners for life. Forever was in their reach.

Maggie closed her eyes and whispered a prayer of thanksgiving for Diana's divine request that had surely been answered. She had found a special man who deserved her love, a man who'd been her best friend for fifteen years.

Later, as they lay sated among tangled sheets, Jake brushed a strand of hair from her cheek. "I'm sorry for not trusting you with my secret, Maggie. It's just that I've always thought you were damn near perfect. I didn't want you to think less of me."

She slipped her leg over his and trailed a finger along his chest. "I'll never think of you as less than perfect, Jake."

As he caressed the curve of her hip with a calloused hand, he gazed at her with honesty glimmering in his eyes. "This cowboy isn't perfect, honey, and I never will be."

"This woman thinks you are. And that's all that matters."

Epilogue

Jake stood in the doorway of Maggie's office, which they'd built just off the kitchen. He watched her sit at the mahogany desk and study the screen of her computer.

"Busy?" he asked.

She looked up and smiled. "Never too busy for you."

He made his way into the room that not only served as an onsite clinic for the kids who attended Buckaroo Ranch, but also as her private study. "What are you doing?"

"Checking e-mail." She swirled in her seat, facing him and revealing the gentle swell where their baby grew. "I've been asked to speak at a pediatric symposium on birth defects in San Antonio next month."

"That's great." Jake was proud of his wife, not only here at the small clinic on the ranch, where more and more families in the surrounding communities brought their children to her for well checks and emergencies, but also because her hands-on experience with cerebral palsy and physical therapy—along with her research—had garnered her a great deal of respect in the medical field. On a weekly basis, doctors and hospitals called to consult with her on difficult cases, and she found herself lecturing around the state. "You won't have to be gone overnight, will you?"

"Not this time."

"Good." He missed her something awful when she was gone. "The kids sleep better when you're home at night."

"The kids?"

He grinned. "Me, too. We all miss you. The family isn't the same when you're gone."

Maggie laughed. "Look at you, Jake. You've become a real family man. At one time, you were afraid you'd make a lousy dad and felt sorry for Sam and Kayla."

"Yeah, but I was wrong about a lot of things, Maggie. And you know what?"

"What?" she asked, standing and making her way toward him. He opened his arms and she stepped into his embrace.

"This family stuff is pretty neat." He kissed her slowly and purposefully. "And I especially like being a husband."

"Hey, Dad?" Kayla asked from the doorway. "Can I ask you a question?"

Jake couldn't remember when Kayla had stopped referring to him as her uncle, but he would never forget the first day she referred to him as her dad. It had sent his heart topsy-turvy. In fact, two years later, it still did. "Sure, honey. Go ahead and ask."

"Where's the carpet cleaner?"

"Carpet cleaner?" Maggie slowly turned from Jake's embrace. "Why, pray tell, do you need carpet cleaner?"

She bit her lip, as though trying to protect someone. And Jake knew exactly who that someone was. Sam wasn't a bad kid; he was just inquisitive and active. And prone to messes and trouble.

"I have to clean something," Kayla said.

"What has Sam done now?" Maggie asked, lifting her brow.

"Well," the little girl said, choosing her wise, seven-year-old words carefully. "It really was an accident, and Oreo is mostly to blame. You don't need to punish Sam. He feels bad enough already."

"Suppose you tell us what happened," Jake suggested. "So we can start with the forgiving process."

"Sam was finger painting. And he thought it would be cool to let Oreo finger paint, too."

"Oh, no," Maggie said, closing her eyes and no doubt imagining doggie prints throughout the house.

With Rosa off this week to celebrate her daughter's graduation from Rice University, Jake and Maggie would be facing the cleanup detail alone.

"Don't worry, Mom," Kayla said. "Oreo is outside now. And Sam knew better than to put her paws in paint. That would have made a super-duper mess."

No doubt. Jake figured the dog must have knocked over the finger paint. Thank goodness the stuff was supposed to wash out with soap and water.

"And?" Maggie prodded.

"Sam put Oreo's tail in blue paint and let her wag all over a piece of paper. But then, Oreo saw Herbie the hamster playing in his little ball. And then Oreo chased Herbie into the living room, all happy and wagging her tail."

"Oh, shoot." Maggie started for the door, but Jake

caught her hand. "What was that you once told me about wanting to balance a family and career?"

Maggie slowly shook her head and sighed as she and Jake followed Kayla back into the living room, both prepared for a mess.

But when they entered the room, Maggie gasped and Jake froze.

Feathery streaks of blue decorated the leather sofa and graced the white walls.

Sam looked up from a big, blue spot on the beige carpet near the hearth, where his efforts had smeared a large splotch the size of a honeydew melon and worked the paint deep into the fibers. His eyes pleaded for understanding.

"Oh, Sam," Maggie said. "You know the rules. No playing with finger paint in the house, unless someone is supervising you."

"But I wasn't playing. Me and Oreo were making a surprise for you. I'm really sorry, Mommy."

Jake bet he was.

Maggie blew out a soft sigh. "I know you are, Sammy. Why don't you and Kayla forget about the mess in the house. Go outside and take a hose to Oreo's tail. Daddy and I will clean this up."

"Okay, Mommy. I'll clean up Oreo, good as new. Come on, Kayla. You can help." Then he flashed Maggie an appreciative grin and tore out of the house, with Kayla on his heels.

Jake laughed and gave his wife's hand a gentle squeeze. "Most moms would be madder than an old wet hen, Maggie. But you've always had a soft spot for bad boys, haven't you?"

"I still do." She wrapped her arms around his neck and kissed him. "Especially bad boys who love me."

Jake wrapped his arms around his wife and kissed her with all the love she had set loose in his heart. He was one lucky cowboy.

A man's life didn't get any better than his.

* * * * *

We hope you love ALMOST PERFECT so much that you share it with friends and family. If you do—or if you belong to a book club—there are questions on the next page that are intended to help you start a book group discussion. We hope these questions inspire you and help you get even more out of the book.

Almost Perfect

by

Judy Duarte

BOOK CLUB
DISCUSSION QUESTIONS

1. While Judy Duarte touches on a number of different issues in ALMOST PERFECT, what is the underlying theme of the book?

2. Jake and Maggie both come from alcoholic and dysfunctional families. How did they react to this challenge? Were their reactions and compensations dissimilar? If so, how?

3. Do you think Jake's and Maggie's relationships with their parents played a part in their reluctance to imagine themselves as part of a family? Do you think childhood experiences determine the type of adult a person becomes? In what ways are adults constrained by their pasts, good and bad? Is it possible for someone to break away from what they have been taught as a child? If so, what types of obstacles may stand in that person's way?

4. Jake spent most of his life avoiding failure. Why do you think failure was so terrifying to him? How did his fear affect his relationships? Why do you think his fear of failure didn't transfer to the rodeo arena or his work with animals?

5. How do you think Jake's decision to return to night school related to his decision to go after Maggie? Do major changes always precede an adult's return to college or vocational school? What types of events might cause someone to seek adult education?

6. Do you think teachers have a powerful effect—positive or negative—on children and the adult selves they become? In what ways can an educational system encourage—or fail—a child?

7. Do you think Kayla's abilities and disabilities influenced Jake's decision to tackle his fear of failure? If so, how?

8. Each character reacted to Kayla's disabilities in a different way. What were some of the positive and negative reactions they displayed? Do you find it difficult to deal with others' disabilities? Why or why not?

9. Maggie used her professionalism as a shield even as her marriage crumbled and she was forced to work with her husband's new wife. Can Maggie's desire for perfection and professionalism be seen as a disability? Why or why not? How did her perfectionism influence her feelings for Jake and Kayla?

10. Maggie felt that being a doctor was part of who she was. How do you think the story might have ended if Jake hadn't needed a pediatrician for his special needs ranch? What other types of sacrifices, besides those related to careers, might men and women need to make for their marriage? Is sacrifice always necessary in a relationship? How do you think sacrifice and compromise affect relationships?

11. Maggie and Jake were close, though long-distance, friends before they were lovers. How did their friendship affect their decision to become intimate? Is it possible for men and women to be close friends without attraction becoming an issue?

12. Do you think Maggie and Jake noticed their attraction to each other in the past? If so, why do you think they never acted on it?

13. At the beginning of the story, Jake has lost his sister, become guardian to his niece and nephew and inherited a ranch. How do these immense changes affect him? Did they open the door for his relationship with Maggie? If so, how?

14. Do you think friendship makes a good foundation for marriage? Why or why not?

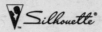

Coming soon only from

SPECIAL EDITION™

The McClouds of MISSISSIPPI

by
GINA WILKINS

After their father's betrayal, the McCloud siblings
hid their broken hearts and drifted apart.
Would one matchmaking little girl be enough
to bridge the distance…and lead them to love?

Don't miss

The Family Plan (SE #1525)
March 2003
When Nathan McCloud adopts a four-year-old, will his sexy
law partner see he's up for more than fun and games?

Conflict of Interest (SE #1531)
April 2003
Gideon McCloud wants only peace and quiet, until
unexpected visitors tempt him with the family of his dreams.

and

Faith, Hope and Family (SE #1538)
May 2003
When Deborah McCloud returns home, will she find her
first, true love waiting with welcoming arms?

Available at your favorite retail outlet. Only from Silhouette Books!

Where love comes alive™

If you enjoyed what you just read,
then we've got an offer you can't resist!

Take 2 bestselling love stories FREE!
Plus get a FREE surprise gift!

COMING NEXT MONTH

#1543 ONE IN A MILLION—Susan Mallery
Hometown Heartbreakers

FBI negotiator Nash Harmon was in town looking for long-lost family, not romance. But meeting Stephanie Wynne, the owner of the B & B where he was staying and a single mother of three, changed his plans. Neither could deny their desires, but would responsibilities to career and family keep them apart?

#1544 THE BABY SURPRISE—Victoria Pade
Baby Times Three

Wildlife photographer Devon Tarlington got the surprise of his life when Keely Gilhooley showed up on his doorstep with a baby. *His* baby. Or so she claimed. Keely was merely doing her job by locating the father of this abandoned infant. She hadn't expected Devon, or the simmering attraction between them....

#1545 THE ONE AND ONLY—Laurie Paige
Seven Devils

There was something mysterious about new to Lost Valley nurse-assistant Shelby Wheeling.... Dynamic doctor Beau Dalton was intrigued as much by her secrets as he was by the woman. Would their mutual desire encourage Shelby to open up, or keep Beau at arm's length?

#1546 HEARD IT THROUGH THE GRAPEVINE—
Teresa Hill

A preacher's daughter was not supposed to be pregnant and alone. But that's exactly what Cathie Baldwin was...until Matthew Monroe, the onetime local bad boy, came along and offered the protection of his name and wealth. But who would protect *him* from falling in love...with Cathie *and* the baby?

#1547 ALASKAN NIGHTS—Judith Lyons

Being trapped in the Alaskan wilds with her charter client was not pilot Winnie Taylor's idea of a good time, no matter how handsome he was. Nor was it Rand Michaels's. For he had to remind himself that as a secret mercenary for Freedom Rings he was here to obtain information...not to fall in love.

#1548 A MOTHER'S SECRET—Pat Warren

Her nephew was in danger. And Sara Morgan had nowhere else to turn but to police detective Graham Kincaid. Now, following a trail left by the kidnapper, would Sara and Graham's journey lead them to the boy...and to each other?